IN TRA

by

David Chaloner

Copyright © David Hamilton Eddy 1983, 2023

The right of David Hamilton Eddy to be identified as author of this work has been asserted by him in accordance with the Copyright, Designs and Patents Act, 1988.

This book is a work of fiction, all characters are the invention of the author, and any resemblance to real persons living or dead is purely coincidental.

This book is sold subject to the condition that it shall not by way of trade or otherwise be lent, resold, hired out or otherwise distributed without the Publisher's written consent in any binding or cover other than that in which it is published without a similar condition to this being imposed on any subsequent purchaser.

A CIP catalogue record is available for this title from the British Library

ISBN: 9798397290845

Cover image: *Starry Night* Vincent van Gogh

www.canonburypress.co.uk

FOREWORD

IN TRANSIT was written in my late thirties at the start of the eighties. It is both a personal book and one that addresses the tensions at that time between what we innocently described as men and women.

It is notionally a sci-fi book - the only one I attempted - though any physics major will find the science pretty ramshackle and more inspired by "Warp speed, Scottie" than any futuristic real technology.

However, as we actually anticipate interplanetary if not interstellar travel future voyagers may find some interest in the following pages. This book is dedicated to them.

"But suppose one should try … to challenge fate, to say: 'If I lose, I shall not pity myself.' Suppose one can create one's own inner tension – then it is not true that there is nothing in man. To take this risk would be an act of faith."
(On 'Ketman' from *The Captive Mind*" by Czeslaw Milosz. Secker & Warburg 1953.

"All autistic children demand that time must stop still. Time is the destroyer of sameness. If sameness is to be preserved, time must stop in its tracks. Therefore the autistic child's world consists only of space. Neither time nor causality exist there, because causality involves a sequence in time where events have to follow one another. In the autistic child's world the chain of events is not conditioned by the causality we know. But since one event does follow another, it must be because of some timeless cosmic law that ordains it. An eternal law. Things happen because they must, not because they are caused.

Time also implies hope. Without time there is no hope but also no disappointment nor the fear that things might get even worse. Hence infantile autism and the cosmic law. Once and for all, and absolutely, it ordains how things must be ordered. Sensible laws can be subjected to sensible revision and hence permit hope to arise. Thus it must be an insensible law that never changes. And the essential content of this law is 'You must never hope that anything can change.'"
(*"On Autism"* by Bruno Bettelheim.)

PART 1

Chapter 1

He got up from his desk, stretching with his hands behind his back and walked out into the garden. Above him the constellation of Eridanus glittered like tiny fragments of chrome strangely suspended in a strong light. However much he gazed at the stars he never tired of finding new ways to describe them. He took another step and the wide fronds of a tree were silhouetted against the brilliant panorama. As his eyes adjusted to the dark he saw the two parallel lines of orange glow worms that marked the nearest path and followed it slowly for a few steps until he reached a small blue light at his feet. He pressed it with his toe. An area of about 1,000 square metres slowly became illuminated by a gentle amber light that was projected by twenty or so of the Chinese lanterns that were interspersed on wires throughout the garden. He leaned against a sturdy magnolia already festooned with its trembling harvest of pink and white blossoms and lit a cigarette. He sniffed appreciatively. The night air was cool and damp.

He knelt down and examined the first green shoots of the potato plants, checking their progress against the small white post that carried the date of planting. A little slow, but then he was trying to use less phosphate, which seemed to inhibit the sugar content of the vegetable. These should be tastier. He walked a little further until he came to another blue light and in a moment another rectangle of yellow light conjoined with the first. As he entered this section he felt the humidity and temperature rise. Metre-high tomato plants already heavy with unripened fruit stood like sentinels supported by thin alloy poles.

"Where are you?"

The voice of his wife was soft and tender in his ear. He replied as softly.

"In the garden. Tomato section. Is dinner ready?"

"Five minutes."

"See you in a moment."

He checked the tomatoes quickly, measuring the diameters of the largest and smallest fruit with a set of callipers that had been set for the purpose in the dark loam. Then he set back to the house switching off the blue lights with his feet without breaking his long stride.

When he entered the kitchen his wife was setting out the plates. She had changed into a light green dress that set off her thick black hair and pale skin. He recognised the food and smiled.

"Steak."

"A treat."

"Why the treat?"

"No particular reason."

"Whenever I think of steak, I think of wine."

"I know, but you know the rules."

They ate the meat slowly, trying to imprint in their memories every subtlety of smell and taste and texture. Then he sipped the soda-water he had poured from the carafe and gazed moodily out into the night. His wife observed his expression but did not ask after his thoughts although she was curious about his reflections.

"Any messages from the crystal ball?"

"All clear at seven o'clock."

It had to be checked every hour. If it wasn't warning bells and lights came on all over the place. She sighed, it was a superfluous question, he knew that she would have told him immediately if there had been anything to report. Then her senses sharpened again, there was no such thing as a superfluous question, nothing was superfluous. Everything was significant. She scolded herself for her egocentricity. He was trying to tell her something. He was worried. Therefore do not ask if he is worried. By asking a superfluous question he was warning her not to ask another superfluous question.

She removed the plates and brought in the next course, fresh pineapple with small portions of thick cream – another treat. Again that vague sense of guilt – was she trying to placate him? She took a silent breath and controlled the first hints of irritation. He smiled again.

"Is this a special day?"

"Yes, I love you."

"After all these years, you finally decided."

"Not so many years."

"Quite a few on board this ship."

She blew him a kiss and began to eat her pineapple. Was it the time thing then? Her raid into the refrigerator for the steak and the cream would have reminded him of time, twice over. Well, if it was that, bring it out into the open; her unconscious knew better than herself – not that one should make a distinction between the two. Hey, slow down. She was supposed to be enjoying the treat. His word not hers.

"I think I'm going to reduce the phosphates on the potatoes the next time around. Should give us a better potato. I think the sugar content is being inhibited."

"Not the lighting?"

"No, the lighting, the ultra-violet is optimum. I know it's the fertiliser ..."

"More fertiliser?"

"No less, I just told you. More time, that's what they need, they've plenty of sewage-compost too. They've plenty of everything. But we're rushing them. They're getting too much water. They need to slow down."

"Like us."

He lit a cigarette and looked at her narrowly.

"Am I coming across tense?"

"A little."

"You mean a lot, you wouldn't worry about a little."

"Well, medium."

"It's to do with time, isn't it?"

She looked at him silently.

"Well, time is something we have plenty of, sweetheart."

She didn't reply but started to clear away the plates. She turned to face her husband.

"Coffee?"

"Please."

He watched the movement of her hips as she walked away from him. He remembered the same mixture of anger and delight and desire when they had first met seven years ago. It had been at a party and he had been having a friendly argument with a small group of people, a little younger than him hence in part the friendliness, and he had seen this dark-haired young woman smiling at him, but there was an edge to the smile, and he had wanted her there and then for it had this aspect to it that they were alone in the universe and it was necessary that they should be one. He didn't meet her for a month after that and a week after their second meeting she had agreed to marry him. So he had always thought that their relationship was to do with speed rather than time. Yes, there had always been a momentum.

He wished he could identify his mood. It felt strange to him. He thought that perhaps it was to do with his age. He had turned forty a few months ago, and small things had become endowed with a new intensity. But there was something else.

There were some things he didn't particularly want to think about, but there was one thing that was clear to him. During the five years that he and his wife had been in their present home he hadn't made a serious mistake or taken any kind of real risk. That was ironic because their entire project was nothing if not risky, but this he had become immune to. No, if he didn't do something risky, if he didn't go a little crazy … then he really would go crazy. Of course he had been warned about this, but even so, even so. He watched his wife come back with the coffee. Funny that he thought of her all the time as "his wife", but to address her by her first name would seem self-conscious. He smiled, charmingly at his wife as she sat opposite him again feeling a vague sense of pleasure at his hypocrisy.

"You look nice in that dress." It was true, he always had felt that the dress had suited her. He remembered buying it with her in Saks.

"How's the coffee?"

"Delicious."

He was breaking all the rules, he was out of control. Not too late to haul back, it would never be too late to haul back. No risk then? No, he could go too far to come back, he knew that now.

"You're so good-looking when you're deep in thought."

He looked into her eyes and knew that she wanted to make love. Perversely, he wanted to make love too. Why perversely, this was ridiculous. He remembered his training. It was natural that there would be occasions when he would want to kick over the traces, he would know when it happened and there were a number of simple things that would be guaranteed to solve the problem, and if some of those techniques didn't work he could always share them with his partner, who in this case happened to be his wife. There was no psychological problem he couldn't lick.

"I'm going to have a look at the screens for a while."

She wanted to say, there's nothing to see I only checked them an hour ago.

"OK, darling, see you soon."

He walked out through the other door, went down a short corridor through another door and started to climb the spiral stairway.

She decided to let whatever was bugging him run its course. After seven years she reckoned she knew her husband pretty well, and that whatever was on his mind would be revealed to her in due course. As he had said they had plenty of time. Anyway, it was more fun to wait.

*******   *******   *******

As always, he felt this sense of peace up here. Even the air smelled fresher – that was purely psychological. He walked over to the window and looked out over the garden. Even today after five years of daily observation it seemed immense. He looked up at the huge glazed canopy that covered the garden and everything within it. Only a faint blue sheen at the horizon of the garden betrayed its existence. Otherwise he might as well have been in space looking directly at the stars. This was the closest he had ever got to a religious experience. Entering the control room was like entering a temple. A temple for the gods, the ancient gods. Here where height and depth had no significance was Mount Olympus. He never felt alone here; rather he was continually caressed by the numinous robes of the Unseen.

In the middle of the room, like a huge raised black tablet supported at each corner by four pillars of charcoal-coloured metal stood the screens. He focused his mind on a certain number, concentrated his thoughts on the centre of the tablet as if it were a mandala and the screens blazed with every colour of the rainbow.

He examined each glowing rectangle, trajectory, speed, gravity control, air mix, air purity, laser shield, radar micro- and macro-scales, field detectors lux and radio, engine states, anti-G motor (or CRADL, co-ordinated retroactive drive levitator), LMI (local mass inhibitor, use not anticipated but you never knew) and IC (for ion control to do with the metabolism of the plants and themselves). There were all the usual temperature and humidity gauges, and the erratic 'pink, pink, pink' of the radioactivity monitor. Wanting information on the AM he concentrated again and a developed AM profile rippled over the central screen. It was perfect. Everything was perfect. With a flick of his mind he turned off the screens.

They were travelling at about ¼c which effectively limited their maximum range to 3 parsecs even allowing for the 'slowing-down' of metabolism at light speeds. In astral terms 3 parsecs was nothing but it brought a sizeable bag of stars to play in. ¼c had been the limit when they had left Earth five years ago, a more powerful nuclear motor would have blow itself and any surrounding vehicle to thousands of tiny radioactive bits. His one major anxiety was that in those intervening five years or indeed within another five or ten years they would have broken yet another tech barrier allowing them to move on up to light speed and beyond in which case they would be overtaken. Every day he checked the detector scans for any sign of pursuit.

And the purpose of this very expensive expedition? Was discovery. The same principle motivated them that had motivated Columbus, da Gama and Marco Polo. The entire purpose of their two lives was restricted to discovering a planet that was as similar to Earth as possible. The chances of discovering such a planet were statistically remote; nevertheless, it had been decided that it would be worth the effort. Their craft was just the first of many probes into deep space. Their task was to find the planet and return with the recorded evidence. The operation could have been handled by the computers and robots onboard. In a sense therefore their true mission was to survive. In all likelihood they would both be dead by the time their ship returned to Earth, but the times of their deaths would have been recorded as would every action and many of their thoughts on the ship's log. And for those who were to follow that could be priceless information.

Strange myths surrounded those astronauts involved in accidents – people whose ships had got out of control, often ending up in freak elliptical orbits that had returned their corpses but also the records of their thoughts, their tormented or tranquil or philosophical or furious thoughts.

Eventually, these doomed creatures had committed suicide or gone mad or starved or flown into a cloud of asteroids. Others, who had in every other way maintained their sanity, had seen apparitions, had communed, apparently, with complete strangers or people they had known on Earth. Some had written poetry.

None of these men or woman had, however, chosen their destiny. Whether singly or collectively they had all inhabited ships that had been out of control. He and his wife on the other hand had accepted the risks and consequences of a lifetime of travelling through space, had prepared for it and trained for it with all the resources that had been available in the wealthiest country in the world. Moreover, he had positively wanted to leave the Earth. This was more real to him than the planet that had given him life. He had wanted to escape from the horde. Not even his wife knew that. He would never have been accepted if the agency had known that. Loner was the dirtiest word in the Agency's book. So he had invested, for the sake of the tests, his few friendships with a false dignity and questioned as to whether he would not miss those social props to his ego (of course, they hadn't put it so bluntly) he had maintained quietly and convincingly that it was precisely the sacred memories of men and woman that he had been *privileged* to know on Earth that would sustain him against the anonymous dark. (He had liked that last phrase.) The night before the final selection he had been sweating so profusely he had had to walk the streets until breakfast time. He hadn't wanted his wife to see the state he was in. When they were informed that they were the couple who had been chosen for the momentous expedition he had wept with relief.

Throughout the selection process he had barely given a thought to his wife's role in the final victory. Instinctively, he had kept discussion of the whole affair to a minimum. He knew she would rise to the challenge, that was enough.

So as he looked through the transparent roof at the stars above, it was this passion that warmed and sustained him – that he was in charge of this machine and nothing and nobody could touch him. He was flying free.

He walked over to the console and pressed the record button. He looked up at the stars again as if seeking inspiration. Then he began to speak quietly but quickly describing his activities and thoughts of the day. Mostly he talked about his work in the garden. He didn't refer to his angry escape from the Earth; he never had, some superstition held him back from recording his thoughts concerning life on Earth. Once, tentatively, he had suggested that more astronauts than people might think were motivated by feelings of, well, even hatred. But her surprised interest, her shining fascination at such a thought had stopped the words in his throat. He was both ashamed and thrilled by the furies and that fired him like the controlled nuclear explosions that fired this ship.

Perhaps that was why he always felt depressed after he had finished his log for the day, like going to confession and never quite telling the entire truth. Well, the hell with it, why should he give them any more. Anyway, what with the still uncertain state of nuclear technology the chances were that the whole ship would go up one day like a huge H-bomb. Not that anyone on Earth was likely to see it, perhaps a bit of crackle on a radio-telescope, the minutest of sparks in the universe. Travelling through space gave you a sense of scale.

The greatest of suns, the ones that imploded like shrinking gas balloons as their nuclear energy failed, all those electrons turned into photons and heat, all those atomic nuclei raining in on each other in an hysterical accumulation of gravity that finally became so intense that nothing could escape its embrace, like a black spider at the center of an unseen web, yes, those dark bitches of black holes that so often hid behind gas clouds just out of reach of their tentacles and so invisible until you flew into them at $\frac{1}{4}c$ and saw the last sight of your life, a universe full of nothing, even those monsters were the smallest of irritants in the great dull, bland everlastingness.

And it seemed now that the only thing filling all that star-backed black stuff outside the plexiglass were his own thoughts, and maybe the thoughts of his wife. He wished he could see those thoughts, maybe his were blue and hers were red, like the towels in the bathroom. Not that they really cared who used what towel.

He grinned, he felt better. He always did after an hour up here. Maybe he would screw his wife after all.

Chapter 2

One of the advantages of travelling at ¼c was that the mass of the ship had increased to a point approximately equivalent to that of the moon. The consequence of this phenomenon was that there was a substantial local gravity to the ship, which made everything much more pleasant. They both exercised on the spring-machine every day for an hour and this maintained their muscle tone. In the reduced gravity their spines had elongated a little and they were both nearly an inch taller than they had been on Earth. Though they had a small pool they found swimming difficult as their bodies floated half out of the water. However, she was delighted to keep her youthful high breasts and to live bra-less. All this, of course, had been anticipated and they had spent several months during their training period acclimatizing on the moon.

Such were his thoughts as he stretched lazily on the big divan in their brightly lit bedroom. The lighting and heating on the ship were related to the Earth so that the experience of day and night, summer and winter were replicated as closely as possible both for their own health and that of the plants. The plexiglass that curved over the entire living area of the ship was tinted blue so that when the main lights were up you couldn't see the stars, only the blue 'sky'.

Pink and grey hologram clouds drifted now against the blue as in an old Hollywood studio set. Sometimes the air cooled to the point where it condensed in a white mist that hung two or three feet above the ground. Sometimes the air became so charged with negative ions that hisses and crackles signalled that sparks were flying around the spaceship in a miniature thunderstorm. The weather had been programmed to do this; IC ensured that the metabolisms of plant and human life got this occasional stimulation. Even the dangers of fire or electrical fault had been calculated. All life forms it had been discovered needed a certain degree of trauma. Plants living in 'perfect' environments eventually died of boredom. So if a small fire in the garden caused the human population to sprint about carrying buckets of water, the resultant burning up of adrenalin was salutary. The point was that the system was deliberately designed not to be perfect, it needed human maintenance; their survival depended on their alertness.

He threw up the cigarette pack once more, watching fascinated as it soared up turning slowly, the bright lights making its colours of blue and white and red glow dizzily. He had argued fiercely for his addiction, citing his excellent health and the longevity of his ancestors, all of whom had been smokers and in the end he had won. There were thousands of packets on board, donated by grateful tobacco companies; though more recently he had taken to growing his own weed, curing it himself in the heat of the lights. It was pretty good, too.

His wife was still asleep beside him. The room was already quite warm – it was practically the middle of summer – even though it was only about eight o'clock. She opened her eyes, which were very blue, and they looked at each other for a while. At times like this they were very conscious of each other's extraordinariness. It was almost as if they were gods to each other, he could pretend that he was Apollo, that she was Venus. Their bodies, so close, seemed immense, every pore, every hair was a mystery. So at times like this they examined each other minutely, trying to see, trying to feel things they had never seen or felt before. He studied an azure tinge on her nether lip as if it were a field of misty bluebells. She looked at his eyelashes and thought of reeds, dark and vibrant at the edge of a green pool. He looked at the curves of her hips and recalled the silver dunes of Carmel, the sand warm and delicate against brown fingers, nails burnished by the sun. She sank her fingers into the muscles of his shoulders and remembered her own feet in gum-boots sinking into Connecticut mud, the gloriousness of that muddy feeling; and he recalled climbing trees as a boy, sliding across the smooth branches, falling naked into some dark lake, had it been a dream ... And so they made love, half awake, half asleep, smells and sensations and memories all interplaying.

And when they came to – a moment of horror. Then they held each other tight and remembered the story of the babes in the wood. And held each other tighter.

Presently, he arose, padded in his bare feet to the kitchen and made fresh orange juice from their own fruit. As he spooned muesli into two bowls he heard a bee buzzing against the window and as an afterthought he put a little honey on top of each pile before pouring on reconstituted powdered milk. One of the things he always missed onboard ship was fresh milk. They had a veritable mountain of powdered milk. They had taken fifty years supply of everything they couldn't grow or produce in some way. He padded back with breakfast.

As they ate she asked what he intended to do that morning. He told her that it was time for routine examination of the nuclear dynamo that provided the electricity for their overall environmental system. Periodic examination of the steam turbine was recommended. This would entail the wearing of his radiation suit. A rather cumbersome process, but it was better to repair things at the first sign of corrosion or wear rather than wait for the red lights to come on. And she? She would check the fruit bushes, collect raspberries and gooseberries for a pie tonight. And check their navigation. She was very good at navigation.

Having agreed their tasks for the morning he donned close-fitting clothes and went to the decontamination room. He entered the little chamber and put on the protective suit. He pressed a button and the elevator took him down three storeys to the turbine room.

He breathed slowly through the air-filter as he entered. The gentle hum was reassuring. The turbine ran on finely made tungsten-chrome bearings lubricated by the toughest oils. It was designed to be maintenance free. However the joints of the steam tubes needed to be checked periodically. In these first five years all that had been required had been a little tightening of nuts as the washers compressed. It was an archaic system with its tubes and nuts and bolts but it was in fact extremely reliable and easy to maintain. Reliable engineering had been an invention of and had been lost with the nineteenth century. He checked the connecting nuts with a wrench and found them all tight with no evidence of leakage. Then he descended another floor and checked the secondary reactor.

Radiation levels in the chamber were well within limit as expected. Core temperature was right on the button. Again he checked the state of all nuts and bolts as well as the electric sensors that warned of any invisible fatigue cracks in the tubing. No cracks. The system was behaving perfectly. It was an engineering jewel. He caressed the core casing gently. He felt moved by its beauty, by the loving care that had gone into its construction. He had known some of the men and women who had worked on it, knew how proud they were of its quality. It was characteristic of him that his unrelenting criticism of the human race softened inasmuch as its members were devoted to quality.

He was a trained engineer as well as being a pilot and he knew that the whole ship was a work of the finest art. Every plastic, every metal was perfectly true and free of impurity and distortion. The most impossible stresses had been thought of and anticipated in the construction. It could ride through anything short of a large asteroid and its computerised scanner could detect man-sized objects billions of miles away.

The energy for all this came from the ten huge main reactors, buried in thousands of tons of lead which helped produce the extraordinarily high local gravitational field – even for the c speeds they maintained. What he was looking at now was a child's toy of a reactor.

The main engines on the other hand were sealed units, connected to the communications center by insulated silver wires through which the pulse rates of the great motors, effectively nuclear explosions, were controlled. Usually, they were propelled by one engine that maintained their speed against cosmic drag and provided the power for their navigational sensors.

Additional motors were activated to power laser weapons that could send their sword-like beams with effective force up to a distance of ten million miles.

They didn't anticipate any aliens, but then any aliens wouldn't necessarily anticipate finding a strange spacecraft.

He clambered back into the elevator, re-entered the decontamination chamber and took a hot shower. The Geiger reading on the suit had been minimal when he had returned from the reactor but he wanted to keep the cumulative count to the lowest possible level – hence the shower. He put on his air force blue sweater and slacks, slipped on black moccasins and rode the elevator back to the house.

******   ******   ******

He watched his wife gardening from the living room window. She was wearing a green top and white shorts that were erotically short and tight. There were times when he liked to pretend that she was a stranger to him, that she had a different personality from the one he knew. This was something he had never discussed with his wife. In a way he felt she knew about his fascination, there were times when they were making love that she grinned, murmuring phrases such as "so you like *that*" and in a way he liked it and in a way he was slightly shocked, as if he were seeing her like another man might see her. He knew that she had had other lovers – before him, and there had been a time when just thinking about them had given a kind of cruelty to his love-making; then he was shocked by her voluptuous response to his coldness. He sensed this was dangerous ground and tended to skirt round it. Sometimes he seemed to catch her smiling at him, but when he questioned her about what made her smile, she laughed it off or told him it was because she loved him and he made her smile. He looked at her buttocks tighten against the shorts as she bent over and felt a luxurious warmth flow through him. She was his woman, entirely his, the nearest other man was light years away.

*******   *******   *******

There are a few male adults who are privileged (or doomed) to fulfil the fantasies of their boyhood. Girls, of course, feed, dress and cuddle their dolls with the realistic expectation that fifteen or twenty years hence they will mother their own children; the only flaw in the continuity being that most dolls are female, thus endowing the male with a suitable mystery for the developing young woman.

Similarly, most boys go through a stage when the most exciting thing they can imagine is to be a fighter pilot or interceptor pilot. Unlike the girls only one or two in a million of the overall population are selected for flight training and only about a third of those get to fly the monstrously fast machines. He had been one of the select band.

He remembered that particular occasion when he had to land his F-42C in a Florida thunderstorm at night. The winds were gusting up to a hundred miles an hour, the airplane was jinking about like he was tobogganing down a slope that was too steep and much too rough; he couldn't see anything except thick cloud all around and purple lightning flashes that threatened to blow off his tail or a wing, there was a torrent of rain on his canopy and the fixes on the auto-pilot VDU kept getting unfixed, he didn't have fuel to reach another base, he estimated that he had ten minutes fuel left, maybe twelve or less than five, all instruments are fallible, and the cloud base was down to two hundred feet. He was scared as hell, but in another way he was exultant, he saw the grandeur of it. This three hundred million dollar interceptor was practically hovering there like some beautiful, huge, evil fucking *bat* and it was out of this world, he was out of this world, and he realised that he was *protected* by this fucking monster, that it didn't give a fuck about tornadoes and VDUs – and he felt his hands take the controls, and the back of his brain was buzzing and electricity was leaping up and down his spine, and his hands knew what to do, and the bat flew in at three hundred knots and the cross of the airstrip lights came up smack in the middle of the windscreen, and the flaps whined down and he went straight as an arrow down the runway. That was when he knew that all he wanted to do for the rest of his life was fly. End of story.

Chapter 3

Whenever she reflected on why she had come she always found it painful. She guessed she was pretty competitive. Captain of the girls' basketball team at White Plains High, captain of the debating society, she had gone out west to study biochemistry and psychology at UCLA eventually taking a master's in cybernetics and math. She seemed to naturally gravitate toward the space programme and spent several months servicing and programming a new environmental system in situ on one of the latest defence orbiting systems. She had a deep feeling even instinct for everything that was practical and possessed a good theoretical mind.

She met her husband at a party in San Francisco, shortly after she had returned from the DOS. He was quite different from the other astronauts she had met. Like other ex-fighter jocks he affected slight disdain for his profession with his insistence at her question that he was a flyer not an astronaut, but there was a humour in his eyes that told her that she had a way to go before she could ring him as just another ego-trip fighter pilot. She would have been more annoyed by his arrogance (it was of that irritating kind that thrives on its own acceptance) were it not for the aspect of solitariness about him. He was convivial even charming to the others but she knew that he was quite alone and that he had paid the price of his detachment. He was of that type that apparently cares practically nothing for the judgements that others might make about his ideas or behaviour and consequently judges himself most severely. She wanted him, yes it was so annoying and irritating right from the start.

When they started in to going out together she was surprised to find that something seemed to be holding him back from her. He told her he wanted her, wanted her as his wife, but there was something wary about him. He reminded her of a wild animal which is uncertain whether to attack or run. Even after she had accepted his proposal of marriage she was bewildered at his occasional unease and suspicions about her commitment to him. Gradually, she realised that these reactions in him were occasioned by his relations with many people, and were both a cause and a consequence of his detachment. Perversely, these attributes of her husband, because they did not disappear with their marriage, served not to alienate her from him but served rather to increase her interest. In fact, when he was overly attentive she usually felt tense and restless. In the end, it worked and they were rarely bored with each other.

When first he told her that he had volunteered for the first interstellar space voyage and wanted that she accompany him, her reaction was not of shock or anger but a sheer inability to grasp the fact the Man had finally decided to fly to the stars and that her husband sincerely wished to devote the rest of his life to this expedition. What was most difficult to comprehend was her husband's conviction that the rest of his life on Earth was insignificant in comparison with a form of existence that to the overwhelming majority of others would be equivalent to suffering solitary confinement for the rest of your days. It had been understood that they would have children one day, did he imagine that she was to have a child on board a spaceship, condemning it, assuming she and her child survived the birth, to a life of imprisonment and premature death. He explained that he would quite understand if she wanted a divorce. She hardly spoke to him for about two weeks after that.

At the end of the two week period she announced that she would go with him, that she was as well qualified as he, and that she thought it appropriate that a man and a woman should explore the stars. Looking astonished at this declaration he made as if to embrace her. Furious, she turned away from him and ran up to the bedroom. She did not want him to see her tears. Half an hour later, dressed in her bra and panties she found her husband gloomy in the darkening lounge. Rubbing her breasts in his face she told him that she wanted to be screwed, now, on the floor.

She remembered now how on other subsequent occasions she had harshly worked her body up against his, as if his flesh were a door through which she could pass to an easier world. She had never experienced that with another man and doubted that she would want it, for sometimes she found herself sobbing in frustration at how trapped he could make her feel - and other times release was so profound that she could not bear to return to the daily round. Finally though, the door remained closed and she was once again on the outside hammering to get in.

*******   *******   *******

No, she still did not really know why she had agreed to go with him, know why he had volunteered in the first place. Their friends, tearfully or angrily had tried to dissuade them. He had furiously declared that it was their own affair that they should get off his back, she had stayed mute, it was a subject that could not be discussed, it was a private matter. Strangely enough, once the Agency had made its positive decision and the national and international media had had their way analysing their lives down to the last iota, after the twentieth or thirtieth television interview, it was a relief to know that in a few days, in a few minutes, in a few seconds one would start the acceleration that would eventually take them up to speeds that Man had never, outside neutron accelerator and radio telescopes, witnessed before let alone personally experienced.

Looking back now it seemed that they had gone through an eclectic form of suicide. The pressure of the acceleration in conjunction with the anti-G drugs and the disorientating effects of CRADL had all contributed to the illusion of dying; so that weeks or was it months after the initial moment of leaving the Earth's surface, when they were finally released from the bonds of G, they found themselves in a world, dreamlike and orderly, that was curiously familiar as if for all their lives they had been preparing for this moment. They had embraced in ecstasy. They were the first human angels.

Actually, the most difficult thing had been leaving her parents. It was not that they had been especially close. Although both her parents had had successful careers – and in computers at that – she never felt that they had been sympathetic to her work. As a child she had been a promising cellist; her teachers had confided to her parents that she had every chance of becoming a concert player.

At seventeen she had given up music – she knew she didn't have the stuff of greatness, and she was not prepared to settle for a good orchestral standard. It was soloist or nothing. Her parents hadn't understood that, they thought she was being indulgent. There were only fifty to a hundred orchestral cellists, musicians who could play with the top professional symphony orchestras. She had riposted that there weren't five soloists, and she knew that she was nowhere close to the three performers she admired. And only one of those was an American. It was the turning point.

The fact that she had gone on to become one of the best environmental systems analysts in the whole of North America seemed only to cause resentment towards her from her parents.

She had an older brother but he had been killed in a sports car when he was twenty-five. That had been the most important thing that had happened in her life, more important than flying to the stars. Her husband didn't know how important, how shattering Joe's death had been, certainly her parents didn't know. Her parents had been stunned of course by their son's death but were unchanged by it, at least to her perception. She, on the other hand, had become a recluse, burying herself in her work – it had happened in the last year of her master's – her only social contacts were getting herself laid, always of course by a different man. Eventually she had sought psychiatric help. She had been lucky and found a man who had been wise enough to intimate that they both knew what she was doing and why, and did she want to go on doing it. She found she did for another six months. Then she was celibate for a year. She had a pleasant affair with an older man, who eventually decided he wanted to marry her. Then she broke it off. She started another casual affair three months into which she met her husband. At which point she ended, with some slight regret, the affair.

After her marriage, her parents' attitude towards her had softened, mainly because they liked their new son-in-law, but at least they had started to communicate again. And then the big decision. She had gone back to the psychiatrist before she had made that decision; that was another thing her husband didn't know. Nor for that matter did the Agency. Her psychiatrist told her that he thought she was crazy to even consider going, any sane person would think her crazy. She ventured that it was possible that it was significantly less crazy than driving a sports car at one hundred and fifty miles an hour at night. He agreed, cautiously, that it was just possible. She had embraced him and left with her decision.

******* ******* *******

"By knowing things that exist, you can know that which does not exist. That is the void."
She sat lotus-fashion in the middle of the garden and meditated on Shinmen Musashi's words from the Book of the Void. She emptied her mind of everything but these words, especially thoughts that interpreted their meaning. The meaning of the words was available directly if one did not struggle to understand. Then she closed her eyes and wiped away Musashi's words so that her mind was empty.
There was no Zen master on board this ship so they had to attend to the one outside. Space itself was henceforth their teacher. They had had to learn to understand that their environment was the best possible environment for their particular destinies. To be travelling in space was as natural as being on the Earth, which was itself travelling through space. The sense of reassuring solidity customary on Earth was mere illusion. God was as much in this manufactured cosmos as in the most enchanted terrestrial forest. Their human society of two was as perfect and fulfilling as a city of twenty million. All their needs were met. They were in paradise or hell depending on their understanding.
Her mind was empty so she did not think these things. Rather it was a level of knowledge that she had reached previously and which sustained

her now without need for ratiocination. It was experienced in a warmth that flowed through her body which felt relaxed and heavy. What sustained her also was the knowledge that she and her husband had taken responsibility for their situation and that in the beauty of the living things that surrounded her and indeed in the delicacy and fineness of the spacecraft itself there was a source of inspiration and wonder that would inspire them in the most difficult times.

But now she felt the presence of somebody behind her, the presence of someone who was troubled. It was her husband. She opened her eyes. Why did he not speak? She felt him standing there silently. She could feel his eyes hungry and burning on her body. She took a slow breath and exhaled slowly. She felt that he wanted to rape her, smelled his cruelty like smoke. She felt her cunt contract while her mind withdrew to a watchful distance. Her thoughts fluttered like the wings of a trapped bird and anger surged up and emanated the signal that she was not to be touched, she was alone, she wanted to be alone. There was a contest of wills, then she felt her husband recede. She sighed and felt irritated as if something had been touched then avoided. She turned around sharply. There was no-one there. In the distance, through the living room window she saw her husband. He was sitting at the table apparently engrossed in a book. She watched him steadily for what seemed a long time, but he did not look in her direction. She got up and wandered back to the house.

He looked up from his book and smiled.

"You look nice."

She didn't reply to this but went over to the water-fountain and bathed her face, then drank from a cupped hand.

"How is the environmental reactor?"

"Good. Not a nut loose. How's the garden?"

"It's fine. I meditated a little."

"Well you look fantastic."

"I'm going to lie down for a while. Will you make lunch?"

"Sure, see you soon."

She retired to the bedroom.

Chapter 4

She lay on the bed and made herself calm down. She tried to think. She remembered how tense she used to feel playing the cello. Everybody had understood that it was to be her profession. She got to feel so tense that she hated the instrument, yet knowing how beautiful it could be. She loved its resonance, the particular timbre with which it had been endowed by its Venetian maker, the thrill she felt when playing certain pieces. For a while she was free of her dull existence back in the eighteenth century playing in some dusty chamber in the late afternoon, the sunlight streaming golden through the open window, Vivaldi tapping the rhythm peremptorily with the toe of his polished slipper. That was what she had dreamed of, to travel through space and time and play in the great orchestras of the world – to be an anonymous part of some wondrous occasion.

Instead she felt that the spirit of the music had been lost – at least in Connecticut. Perhaps she had been unlucky; if she had had different teachers, met different musicians, her life might have been different. But that was speculation. Her gifts such as they were had died on the branch. Now she was in reality part of a wondrous occasion, young women in the future would sigh and dream of being the first to travel to the stars and hers would be a name to conjure with, one of the immortals. And she just felt numb.

Sometimes in these low moods she would play Mozart or Brahms on the stereo. It took her back to her childhood, that peculiar moody atmosphere of childhood.

Sometimes listening to the clarity of Bach she felt the glory of sweeping through the universe in this fast-flying bird, and sometimes she felt so tense she could hardly breathe, she felt so claustrophobic. In these moods, everything that was in the ship was exactly that – a thing, an object that may have had its particular reason for being there but each time you used it or looked at it, it lost a little of its magic, its truth, whether it was the most magnificent symphony, the finest painting. They were just objects, dead things, distractions from the vast nothingness through which they flew.

On the little table beside their bed stood a model of her husband's old interceptor, a F42C. She remembered him carving it out of wood, painstakingly, during the second or third year of their mission. It was painted in Air Force colours and insignia, for ever climbing up to the stars. He had worked on it for hours, whittling and polishing and assembling, working as he always worked with the single-minded, deep-breathing concentration of the child.

In those years such a concentration seemed to be of the essence of their future. They had learned the arts of navigation, of developing their garden, of balancing the air mixture correctly. They had learned how important apparently minor details of humidity and ionisation could be. They felt like gardeners and carpenters putting the finishing touches to some ancient baroque palace. She remembered the gardeners in *"Alice in Wonderland"* painting the flowers.

Only gradually did they realise that this process of production had come to an end. It was like that point in making a movie when the actors and technicians had gone and the editor and director were running through the film over and over again, working out what to keep, what was of the authentic picture. This was where the picture was made, in this simple process of cutting and sticking; the picture was made by what you discarded as much as by what you kept. Beforehand, you have the pleasure of seeing the completed movie in the cinema or on television. It would be the same for her and her husband. On Earth there was the thrill of preparation, the incalculable implications of flying to the stars, the construction of the mighty film set that was their spacecraft for the two actors that were them. And one day, people would write the story of their flight, would explain how heroic and epic it was. And she supposed it was heroic and epic, but she also knew that the before and after are always lies, and it is only the now that is true, it is just sticking one bit of experience on to the next – or discarding thoughts because they are pointless, they don't lead anywhere.

So the most important thing was that their life together should be true – no matter what the consequences of that truth should be; because here there was no money, no power, no fame. There was only the truth – or lies.

She loosened her shorts and touched herself tentatively. Pleasure radiated warmly through her body. One of her lovers had entered the room. She remembered how he had looked playing tennis. Her fingers moved firmly; she saw him standing at the foot of the bed. She could see the shape of his erect prick inside his tennis shorts. She smiled, she was dressed for tennis. She watched fascinated as he unzipped himself, licked her dry lips at the sight of it, upright and purple, tremoring slightly. His hands were harsh on her hips and she came, calling out lightly with delight. It was Bill.

She awoke to find her husband sitting on the edge of the bed. She looked at him briefly and closed her eyes again.

"What time is it?"

"Six."

She lay motionless for a while. She felt her husband move slightly toward her, smelled his odour, pleasant in her nostrils.

"I'd love some coffee."

"Sure thing."

The bed bounced as he got up and went into the kitchen. She opened her eyes and stared at the ceiling. She examined her feelings – was she depressed? She thought not. Quite calm. She didn't feel guilty. There was nothing to feel guilty about. She picked up a book and began to read while she listened to her husband preparing coffee in the kitchen. Her husband returned with coffee and cookies. She sipped her coffee and ate a cookie.

"May I have a cigarette?"

"I thought you'd given up."

Anger stabbed through her again. This wasn't going to be so easy.

"One cigarette won't kill me."

He gave her a cigarette and lit it for her.

"Thanks."

More silence.

"Are you OK?"

"Sure, I'm fine."

"You look a little tired."

She sighed.

"Yes, it's always a mistake to go to bed in the afternoon."

She looked at him through the cigarette smoke. His eyes were very neutral. He was controlling his anxiety. She was always impressed the way he could do that. She didn't think she was so good at it. She could feel him sensing her. She made herself transparent.

"Well, the reactor's fine."

She smiled.

"Yes, you said." She took another sip of coffee.

"What were you reading?"

"Test Pilot."

"Not again!"

"Great book."

"Yes, well. OK husband, I'm going to have a bath, go upstairs then cook your supper. Something dull like beans and rice."

"I shall return to my book."

Ten minutes later she was soaking in the tub and he was sitting on the sofa reading. Every now and again his concentration lapsed and he had to re-read the page he'd just finished. Maybe he was getting bored with it; if he'd read the book once, he'd read it twenty times.

*******   *******   *******

He threw the book down, looking at his watch. It was early evening. He walked out into the garden. The first stars were beginning to appear. He switched on the lanterns in the fruit area and examined the blackcurrant bushes. The berries were ripe, dusky and full. A slight breeze riffled the upper leaves of the bushes. The fans had come on. He picked up a shallow fruit basket and began to collect berries. In half an hour he had filled the pannier.

He lay on his back and looked up at the sky. The stars were twinkling strongly now. The feeling of oppression had returned. He could not understand why he felt so disconsolate. After five years he felt they had left behind the melancholia they had been warned about. Apparently not.

It was frustrating, he had made the ship his own, had trained himself to accept the limitations of the vehicle. He sighed, turned over and did fifty quick press-ups. He felt a little better after his exertions.

It was the absence of the unexpected. That was the problem. But one thing was clear. There had been Life before Launch and Life after Launch, and they were completely different modes of experience. Drinking a Budweiser on LBL at home alone was not an entirely solitary activity. Sipping a Bud you automatically thought of the times when you had shared a six-pack with buddies and the times you would in the future. Therefore on LAL there was a kind of anguish to having a beer called Budweiser, it was like you were banging a nail into the coffin of a friend. You could drink the Bud but you went through this rigmarole, like here comes this obvious misery and you can get yourself above it by fighting the battle between the obvious and the subtle. That really characterised LAL, you had to keep cheating the obvious reaction to things. It was a matter of self-discipline, of overcoming your fear of claustrophobia, or boredom, or nothingness or whatever. And it was extraordinary how possible it was to beat the obvious, how good one could become at it. In one sense it was merely the continuation of a process that had started when he had trained as a fast-jet military pilot, controlling your reactions to the unusual or unexpected, after all that was what the word *training* meant – but of course in another sense it was all on an utterly different plane.

Before he had taken this trip he had never picked fruit in a basket, had never gardened, had never used a spade. Sure, they had had apples and plums in their place but it was all very casual and laid-back. If you needed fruit you went to the supermart – it was all so cheap. And then a few metres away an attractive young woman who was his wife was navigating a monstrously large and expensive spaceship through the heavens at something over a quarter the speed of light. And this was, had to be, perfectly normal and everyday. If it wasn't perfectly normal and everyday you went crazy. People had used to work down a coal mine for twelve, sixteen hours a day, adolescent girls worked sixteen, eighteen hours a day in the sweat-shops of the garment industry. In many parts of the world they still did. They always would. That was one of the reasons he had left the Earth, to leave *that* and find more space. Hell, he was living in the lap of luxury. It was Paradise. Just keep thinking that.

A lot of the fruit was ripening at the moment, they would have to freeze it. It was difficult to get the balance right between production and consumption. They had a horror of starvation and tended to overproduce.

With all this ripening fruit the garden had a heavy, brooding quality; the air was too scented, it was beginning to smell like a greengrocers.

They had plenty of meat, refrigeration in space was no problem – the size of the refrigerator in which they were flying was infinite. But he missed not having wine. It would have been easy to make alcohol on board, but as on board ship, alcohol was taboo. All forms of stimulants or drugs were taboo. Before taking the trip they had their appendices removed. Dental caries was a thing of the past but they had been taught how to care for their gums. Both were adepts in shiatsu and acupuncture. Prevention of illness was the key to health.

Here time had to be your friend. You had to be able to sit in a certain spot for days at a time doing nothing but stare at a single object – it might be a star, it might be an apple hanging from a tree. You did that for a few days and afterwards, when you moved around the ship again, you would be amazed at how much had changed, in the garden, on the data bank, in your wife's face. Doing nothing was a way to seeing much.

He lit a cigarette, inhaled deeply. One day he would have to stop this habit. He was curious as to how his body would handle it. Well, all in good time. He picked up the pannier of fruit and walked back to the kitchen.

Chapter 5

It was not true that space was empty. Of course, it was almost entirely free of gross phenomena such as asteroids, large gas clouds and general debris. But it was saturated with infinitesimally low levels of background radiation, there were particles like neutrinos darting around, the faintest echoes of gravitational fields which would hardly ruffle the electronic feathers of the odd hydrogen atom floating in solitary grandeur and all kinds of itsy-bitsy invisible plasmas that added up to the fact that to the initiated space was a black sauce gently stirred by semi-magical currents that drifted through the universe. Move your hand slowly in water and you hardly feel a thing; dive from fifty feet in the same water and it will feel very hard indeed. You don't feel much travelling at ¼c either, space is pretty empty, but ¼c is a thousand times as fast as the speeds reached by the earliest space rockets, and for comparison's sake there is a big difference between one mile an hour and a thousand miles an hour. Occasionally, for example the ship would go through some kind of sub-plasma cloud and for an hour or two or even a day or two the ship would be surrounded by a beautiful blue-green aura.

The trajectory of the ship could be affected by the contingencies of the spatial soup or by irregularities in its propulsion system. Both these navigational distortions were accounted for by computers but it was wise to check the trajectory daily.

This was her role and in the five years of their voyage there hadn't been a flaw in the process. The directional sensors were firmly locked on to eEridani a star that was approximately 10.8 light years from Earth in the constellation of Eridanus; it had been selected for light and mass characteristics that were similar to those of the sun. At ¼c it would take them over forty years to reach their target, however the relative slowing down of time predicted at sub-light speeds would effectively mean they would be in late middle age when they reached eEridani. If they made it back to Earth their bodies would be those of nonagenarians, though chronologically their ages would be somewhat more or less than 110 years. On the other hand no-one really knew how their bodies would react over 85 Earth years.

If there were not suitable planets around eEridani they would swing back for home. It was between 20 to 50 to 1 that they would find a big, fat white sun with nothing around it at all. Success was to get there; to find a planet like the Earth was in the realms of the miraculous. This had been carefully explained to them over the months of preparation. Equally, any planets they did find had to be explored minutely, including landing where possible – decisions on this would be made within the context of being able to bring the information back home. There was absolutely no point in getting sucked into some planetary bog or drowning in some planetary sea. Anything was possible, they might be overtaken by a faster ship en route or on their return. They might meet a star-jumping colonising ship, a community wandering through the solar system with no intention of returning to Earth. Yes, over the years they had to be ready for anything. In the meantime, their destination was codenamed Esther.

So each day she would plot their course and check the electronic records as to the consistency and currents of the black soup of space. Similarly any objective phenomenon however minuscule that came into the range of their scanners had to be investigated as far as was possible,

She, more than her husband, was the eyes and ears of the ship. Women, it had been discovered back in the sixties of the twentieth century were both more sensitive and more thorough than men. With her musical and mathematical background she was a superb navigator. In any "confrontational situation" however her husband would take over. Hence, her husband did a share of navigation and theoretically at least they consulted continually about the state of things navigational. But practically, her husband was more of an engineer than a navigator. Nevertheless, despite much of the evidence to the contrary he still saw himself as the pilot of the ship.

She sighed and touched the rear view scan button. A circular image of the receding heavens sparkled on the screen. She pressed another button and the programmed star analysis locked on to the image. The machine started to hum, a bright, white line spiralled out from the center. A red dot blinked on the screen and she pressed another button. Another image appeared, the red dot in the center of the screen. She pressed five more times until the red dot had disappeared. She studied the area around the dot. A gas-cloud. She tapped out instructions on the keyboard, there was a second's pause and the red dot went out. She reverted to the original image and again watched the white line spiralling outwards. Another red dot appeared and she repeated the magnification process. Another gas cloud. She continued until the circular image had been covered by the spiralling white line. Then she went through it all again with the forward view scan. Nothing very much was happening, but then in a thousand years the universe changed very little, in a day the changes were practically negligible.

Anyway, there was nothing significant in their path and there was nothing following them. She sighed again and looked up at the stars, slowly pulling her fingers through her hair. They had a lot of leeway.

She sat back in her chair and continued to fiddle with her hair. Why was she feeling so restless and antagonistic? Her period wasn't due for two more weeks. And she had this feeling of being watched. Paranoia. Classical symptoms of paranoia. Five years out and it begins to get to you. She was bored so she was looking for trouble. At times like this it was really a question of pulling yourself together – otherwise you really do go crazy. She would find a new dress – she had brought hundreds – and cook a stylish dinner.

She hurried to the bedroom, riffled through her clothes and selected a strapless red dress cut in the style of the 1940s. She pulled on sheer grey stockings and garters – no other underwear - stepped into red high-heeled shoes and slipped into the dress. She made up carefully.

Chapter 6

He looked up at a bedroom window that was full of stars. His wife was sleeping peacefully beside him. It had been obvious when she had appeared in that tight red dress at dinner that they would fuck in the near future. In the end, halfway through dessert she had knelt on the table, pulled up her dress and waited. The next ten minutes had been a wild confusion of spilled food and drink, torn clothes, obscene imprecations with obscene consequences; eventually they had skidded into a corner of the room where consummation was coldly pleasurable. Afterwards they had lain semi-conscious in the messy results of their abandon. They had showered and fallen into bed. They would clean up the kitchen on the following day.

He had never seen his wife like that before. Tonight she was a stranger to him. Now, he felt alienated and depressed.

He looked at the window. Just stars. No sun, moon or planets. Their sun was indistinguishable from a thousand other bright stars. The rest of their lives lost in the stars; never to see again the breakers on the beach, children playing, having a drink with his wife at sunset after the last swim of the day. At the time he had only seen the bad things, he had never seen the miraculous, the marvellous in the ordinary, everyday aspects of life.

He had had these moods before, but never with this sense of agony and loss. Memories or desires gnawed at his flesh, at his intestines like crabs or rats; he felt the bites of small hard teeth, the sickening pull and release, sucking pull and release of each remorseless memory, crowded and busy on his exposed entrails.

Everything was becoming inimical in this shining and savage world. The radio-active motors, the weaponry, both of which could turn in on themselves in a horror of nuclear fission, their recycling life-support system which could so easily transform their home into a death-camp for two, his wife who was evidently reverting to the predatory bitch that had so perversely attracted him at the outset of their relationship, even his own thoughts and memories had their peculiarly carnivorous enthusiasm.

He got out of bed and walked naked through the spaceship. He felt like a caged animal, restlessly pacing the grounds of its enclosure in a neurotic pattern, repeated thousands of times with that fast, elegant movement of a panther or a jaguar. This was his kingdom, his universe, how proud he had been in the early months, even early years of their voyage. He recalled the deep melancholy, the expiation of some formless doom that drove Jules Verne's Captain Nemo, or Melville's Ahab! Who were they, these miserable voyagers, who sacrificed everything that was natural and even civilised for the power that came of some infernal machine, these Fausts who had pulled at Mephisto's sleeve when they should have held their breath and said a silent prayer as *he* had slid by. The Ship of Fools, The Flying Dutchman, the ship of the Ancient Mariner were vessels manned by ghosts, creatures who were half alive and half-dead, struggling in some limbo.

Yes, that was the position of he and his wife exactly. They had accepted a kind of half-life. Any individual determined to live fully in the world would have killed themselves rather than suffer this disease of a perverted existence. He and his wife had embraced a kind of evil for the sake of some distantly abstract good. That was why she had hated him for asking her to go with him He had demanded that she commit a kind of suicide – and that was one of the ultimate crimes, he had always believed it. What furies had pricked him, had burned him, to put the world, his world and her world, to the flames. No, her decision had been her own. She had her own furies. That was why he loved her.

That was why he still loved her, for there was a love between the condemned, whether they have been condemned to be intelligent or criminal, not that the two were mutually exclusive. Or independent. What a strange description of a human being. No animal or plant could be seen, let alone admired as "independent"! They had followed the myth of the modern age, they had wanted to be independent, to be free, to be … angels! Angels of technology. Yes. Oh, yeah!

And that was all? Was that really all? Dare he think there could possibly be *any* redemptive features, was it really all vanity, his and hers, or was it just … fate? Just fate, just their destiny, not to be examined or criticised. Accept your fate. That was what his wife had learned to do; she had taken the poisoned chalice, drunk and accepted the long and lingering … life. It was he that was fussing and chafing.

He looked around him and found that he was at the foot of a large apple tree. It must have been ten metres high. Suddenly he felt tired and on an impulse lay out on his back on the dark Earth and gazed up at the green boughs, heavy with clusters of unripened fruit. The coolness of the Earth was calming on his bare skin and he reflected on the facts of this cultivated by also natural fragment of Earthly soil whizzing through space in its spaceship casket. He looked again at the shapes of the apples etched against starlight and fell asleep.

He was walking on pink sand. A few feet away from him curious, inky blue waves sucked plaintively at the sand, depositing the usual litter of seaweed and shells. Fifty metres away a grey dolphin leaped high out of the blue foam of the surf. A strong breeze tore at his hair. The surf boomed. Blue and white sea birds hung on the breeze inches from his face. Feathers shiny like silk.

It felt strange and so familiar. The air was good to breathe. Tiny fragments of ice crystals glinted as they were rushed along by the wind. And yet the heat of the sun was such that one did not feel cold. It was appropriate to walk naked along the beach. Inland, trees that looked very like cedars tossed their green manes.

Among the small bushes that came down to the beach hundreds of rabbits nibbled at the green grass that covered the soil. When he walked among them they hopped casually away, giving him a berth of a few metres but otherwise scarcely noticing him.

Among the cedars, it felt much hotter. High, brownish grass like elephant grass surged and billowed hypnotically in the wind. He could see no other sign of life. Then almost indistinguishable from the continual movement of the plain he thought he detected the more purposeful flow of a herd of large animals, though they were too far away for him to gauge whether they were more like antelope than horses. Suddenly they were gone and he wondered if he had imagined them. High in the deep blue sky the sun glinted reddish on the wings of an eagle or buzzard. Then that, too, disappeared.

He decided that he would walk into the long grass. As he walked the hay pulled at his legs, got caught between his toes. It was warm and dry, not uncomfortable at all. He walked for quite a while until he came to an area where the grass did not grow. It was rocky interspersed with gravel. One of the larger stones caught his eye. It seemed to have an inscription on it. He knelt down to examine the marks carefully. They were hieroglyphs.

He awoke to the buzzing of bees and the vegetable smells of the garden. His body was dusty with dried Earth and stiff. He yawned and stretched. He walked over to the bedroom window and looked in. His wife was still asleep, her short dark hair turned toward him. Beyond her head on the same pillow was the head of a man with reddish hair. He could make out his nose and mouth.

He froze, heart racing, then rushed silently into the house, silently into the bedroom. His wife was turning over in her sleep. There was no-one else in the bed. At that moment his wife opened her eyes. She looked calmly at her husband for a second and then her expression changed.

"What's the matter? You look terrible and you're covered in … ." She sat up in bed, furious. "What have you been doing?"

His heart slowed down. He forced a grin. His face felt like a rubber mask. He felt nauseous.

"I fell asleep in the garden. I'll have a bath."

She shook her head in disbelief and buried herself in the sheets. He walked toward the bathroom. En route, he caught a glimpse of the chaos of the kitchen, of the night before. A fear watched down on him from some small upstairs room of the mind. In the bath he bent forward immersing his head in the water and prayed.

Chapter 7

They didn't speak with each other much for days. The process of change in a relationship is slow; it happens remorselessly, but it never appears to be happening. What they had in common was a sense of being watched; of course, since this was the last thing that each was likely to communicate, neither knew this about the other.

They were a distinctive couple; they had left a domain behind them, it was possible they were approaching another. They were only representatives of their species in a certain sector of space, which seemed pretty empty; they didn't appear to be treading on anybody's toes. But they felt less alone than before and it wasn't a comfortable experience. He wouldn't have put it like that. He thought he was getting paranoid.

He seemed to spend more time in the garden. He thought there was no harm in that except that he was more nervous of going to the irradiated areas. He had never been nervous before and he was determined to get to the bottom of it.

He knew what drawing fire meant. In exercise and actual combat as a fighter-bomber pilot he had flown over enemy lines higher than his comrades to distract the opposing missile batteries and guns. It was an uneasy feeling, not dissimilar to venturing into a hostile neighborhood and realising that it is the wrong time of night, that one's clothes, far from extravagant, are yet way too noticeable. Somber eyes, it seems, are watching you and you are putting out a lot of energy saying really quite complex ideas like I'm not looking for trouble, it's a pleasant night, but if trouble came there could be unpredictable consequences and who needs unpredictable consequences. Yes, there is some magic and superstition in combat flying and when you put yourself out on a limb you feel the bough creaking and the eyes on you.

So he was checking every seam in his radiation suit, examining the residual radiation on his skin after stripping the suit, then again after the shower. In the reactor chamber itself he stared at the reactor and its assorted tubes gloomily. Periodically, new plutonium rods had to be inserted. This was a fully automated process, the old rods being vaporised by laser then dumped as a radio-active cloud in space. So far, replenishment had proceeded smoothly. But next time anything could happen.

He spent more time meditating or at least being alone. Conversation with his wife was limited to practical matters of their mutual survival. Some sense advised her not to question him about his present attitude towards her. She recognised that he needed to be alone. Yes, he wanted to be alone.

He stayed long whiles under the apple tree. He felt comfortable there, perhaps because it reminded him of his childhood home in California. There had been an apple tree with a swing. He remembered swinging on that tree for hours daytime and night-time. At night, in the summer, he had sat on the swing-seat, motionless, gazing at the star-lit sky beyond the uppermost leaves of the tree. If he moved then the stars and moon swung crazily, and the sounds of the night birds and the rustle of the wind and the creaking of the rope intoxicated him with a sultriness he had always aimed to recapture.

And sitting under this other apple tree he realised that the sultriness was here too, that just being there invoked that same boyish mood when everything was possible and adventure beckoned from every twist in a country road and any corner of a little town.

He wanted to speak with his wife but feared to do so. He could not forget the expression in her eyes when he had stumbled into the bedroom. He did not want that she should think him crazy. Once she thought that he was liable to see things, well, that was the end. He was the captain of the ship. If captains saw things, they kept it to themselves. And prayed. And had the sense of being watched.

She vacillated between common sense and horror. She did not know the rules concerning her husband's sanity – or her own. Bill had not reappeared but she could feel his presence. What was so strange was that Bill had been practically insignificant to her before. As if offended at her cool treatment of him he was now pestering her. He seemed to be implying that she had used him in some way. That was really ridiculous. She was angry with him, angrier than with her husband.

Then one night he visited her in the bedroom while her husband was writing up the log. She scolded him.

"Why are you here? You've no right to trouble me."

"I have every right. I wanted you and you wanted me. You gave me up because you met *him* and because I knew you too well."

"What do you mean? You know nothing about me."

"I know everything about you. I know how despicable you are."

"Despicable yourself! Who are you to judge me?"

"I know the truth about you, what you really want."

Her heart was pounding.

"What do I want?"

Bill smiled and disappeared. Try as she could she had been unable to conjure him up. She worried that her husband would sense Bill's rather rank smell on the sheets, but if he did he never showed it. She always was checking to see if he had left one of his red hairs. She was fascinated by their colour of red-gold. She would crawl on her hand and knees over the sheets looking for red hairs.

Chapter 8

A week or so after these traumatic incidents he had what he thought was a brilliant idea. They should try to recall and subsequently record every aspect of their lives on Earth beginning with their earliest memories. Almost immediately she agreed that it was a wonderful notion. Here was a way to lay the ghosts of the Bills she had known – all those personages she had lit upon but never fully appropriated, people she had known in childhood whom she had wanted to feel and touch so much more intimately. She hungered to rediscover those she had so casually let slip through her fingers.

This was why she responded so enthusiastically to her husband. Once again she realised why she had been so attracted to him, why she had embraced his presence right from the start with such rapacious devotion. He was so clever.

They had been gardening together when he had broached the idea. The tenderness she instinctively felt towards her husband had been frustrated for weeks, and now, without thinking, she lay on her back, lifted her skirt and passionately beseeched him to embrace her. She felt such happiness as his mouth caressed and sucked, she knew that she had been party, however indirectly, to wounding his ego and now she wanted to use her body as a healing salve. She gave herself up to him telling him over and over again how very much she loved him, how sorry she was if she had hurt him in any way, all the time moving her buttocks against his clever tongue.

It was as if another world had opened up for them. Every day for two, three or four hours they wrote in silence, later showing the results to one another as if they were sacred documents.

They recorded not only the incidents and personages of their childish and adult lives but also what they now saw as significant behind the appearances. Such and such a person was more wise, more tolerant than had been recognised at the age of eight or nine. Faces were evoked once more and assembled on the screens of their memories. Houses were reconstructed, corridors and bedrooms revealed themselves as in an underwater city. They swam through the corridors and rooms like fish.

Imperceptibly, as they entered this world of childhood they became like children. They whispered in each other's ears with the magic of the child's whisper. In each other's faces they saw the child each had been, and if they made love in such moments it was in the spirit of the tense and delighted naughtiness of children. The intimacy of the naughty was like a wrapped gift handed back and forth in an ecstasy of frustration until the surprised 'oh' of spilt orgasm.

Memories now became the reality of their lives. The normal work of the spacecraft became like a dream. At such moments, they stumbled and mishandled the equipment as if feverish or intoxicated. They could not wait to get back to their "records". The relief of their escape from their fears was manifest in their blissful expressions.

He, for example, might recall such and such an incident, that night twenty years before when he and his brother on a motorcycle trip up in Oregon had had to walk ten miles through torrential rain along a forest road. Fifty yards ahead of them a hot blue spur of lightning had brought down half a pine with a crash that shook the ground and a startled doe and her fawn had careened past, grey blurs in the night. They had walked stolidly, protected from the rain by their motorcycle clothing and helmets, pretending they were Vikings travelling through some Teutonic wood. He smelled the burning smell as they passed the shattered tree and he hungered to be there again. By describing every detail he could remember to his wife he was able to transport himself back. But with greater intensity. The expression on his brother's face, his own feet hot in sheepskin lined boots trudging along, the buckles tinkling – this was a scene he could play and replay until every detail sparkled. Memories became pictures he could paint, adding colour and line with each caress of his wife's hair against his face, every soft compression of her mouth as if in the investigation of her body he would find the clues to the recreation of the past. And there was the continual obligato of the murmur of her echoing voice and the scratching of her pencil as she wrote, ensuring that the precious souvenirs were captured for ever.

Indeed, it seemed insufferable that such an occurrence, so evocative of other occurrences involving woods, rain, motorcycles, wild animals and so on so capable of knitting together the strands of time and place, should not be valued properly. Their personal histories were perhaps unexceptional but under the pressure of their investigations they began to understand how crudely they had managed their lives on Earth. Who was to say, it dawned on them, that any one life was exceptional or not. It was just that they had been the most incredible spendthrifts. Everything had been accepted and then lost, without appreciation, like spoilt children neglecting an endless succession of toys.

Each had a different technique. She preferred to work from her dreams, seeing how a particular dream would be associated with certain memories, which would in turn be associated with others. So she would proceed almost erotically with little cries of delight as one memory intensified the pleasure of discovering the next. Sometimes he felt irritated by her gleeful and haphazard jumping from one delicious evocation to another, it lacked order; but she teased him for his seriousness and he backed off from disagreement. This was not a competition he reminded himself and tried to smile tenderly at her bubbling enthusiasm. He had never seen her so happy.

After a while it became necessary to file their memories under different categories. Patterns began to emerge.

The principal sets were science, nature, culture and sex. Sex was a kind of super-set because it was like a glue sticking different types of experience together. Sex was a kind of device that man had invented to raise an interest in all kinds of important but dull areas of life. For example, the fact that they still wore clothes was extremely interesting. A process of intensification.

There were overall metaphorical patterns as well. His memories more often than not had an idea of movement to them, hers were more textural, more social, to do with relations and connections between people and things.

In what seemed to be a very short period of time they had built up a vast documentation on what they were now beginning to call their previous lives. The more they recorded the more there seemed to be to record. It seemed that they had each lived several lives on Earth, had inhabited more than one person. In comparing different sexual experiences it hardly seemed credible that they had been the same people throughout. "But how could you ...?" became the accompaniment to descriptions of various adventures. Increasingly it appeared that far from being the steady characters they had prided themselves on they were perverse and opportunistic creatures, only too ready to mould themselves to whatever contingencies arose.

What was in fact consistent was the mythology of their own consistency. That had changed very little from the earliest years. And this was guarded savagely, this clear picture of the self.

And then a thought had struck them. What were they to make of their present life, this new life of objective investigation and psychological science. How could you analyse a life of analysis?

This sour note was appropriately heralded by a foul smell that suddenly permeated the spacecraft. Rushing to the control room, they were immediately apprised of the fact that the recycling system – foolproof – was breaking down fast.

Chapter 9

There are two fundamental processes in the vegetable domain; they are growth and decay. Growth is associated with photosynthesis which is a process involving the production of carbohydrates from water and carbon dioxide through the mediation of proteins with the by-product of oxygen upon which in turn animal life is dependent. Light is the catalytic agent for this process.

Decay or rotting is the reversal of this process, breaking down the products of growth and hence creating water, carbon dioxide and other chemicals but especially sulphur based compounds and alcohol. Oxygen is used up in this process which is effected best in the dark away from the nurturing influence of light. Decay often follows disease which interferes through bacteria with the growth process. Once rotting takes hold of an eco-system it may be difficult to stop, decay inhibiting growth and so producing more decay. Eventually, the vegetable system becomes a poisonous swamp in which nothing can grow until through drainage or evaporation of the excess water growth can recommence by photosynthesis. The history of the world is an everlasting war between these two states. Growth has been dominant in the world, the vegetable system being sufficiently large to support itself but also the parasitic animal system, the largest component of which was Man. In recent years there had been signs that this particular parasitic component had begun to make ecological demands that threatened to overwhelm the vegetable system.

The success of the spaceship's ecological system, as was increasingly the case with the Earth also, was inextricably linked to a kind of benign interference which ensured that the rotting mechanism should never get out of hand. Disease, for example, operating on fallen ripe fruit consequently poisoning the roots of the plants and so causing the plants to rot would lay the proper basis of swamp creation.

In this case, the benign interference depended upon the control of humidity and the consumption or destruction of ripe fruit. Large areas of the garden had been blighted by rotting apples, and this in turn had affected the "taking up" of their sewage-compost products from the irrigation system. This, of course, only hastened the rotting process and was the source of the bad smell.

There began a period of frantic activity. The "swamp" had to be drained, the excess water separated out from the process before the eco-system could regenerate itself under photosynthesis. Water had to be removed from the atmosphere and from the ground through draining without damaging the still healthy areas of the garden.

Increased activity on their part used up oxygen and produced carbon dioxide that was in excess to what could be absorbed by the damaged vegetable system. Time had in some sense previously been either their friend (it allowed them to do what they wanted) or their enemy (they didn't know what they wanted to do, they were bored). Time had been an ambiguous notion; now it was fickle, it threatened to run out on them. Then, they might run out of time.

They cut off the irrigation systems to all the blighted areas. It was a delicate matter because the most efficient oxygen producers were chlorophyll-rich tropical plants and trees. They had to dry out the evil-smelling base, remove any decayed matter, transport it to compost, replant with seedlings once the ground had dried to the right humidity and pray.

What they were doing, he realised as he staggered along pushing a wheelbarrow full of putrid tomatoes, roots and slimy ferns and rushes, was to encapsulate the process of autumn, winter and spring into a few weeks. The extractors were humming, stealing the humidity out of the air and putting it back into the ship's tanks. The compost trays were like ovens dehydrating the ruined harvest they were shovelling into them.

The heat was terrific. They worked naked, not daring to stop. The oxygen level was steadily falling and had to be replenished from the emergency tanks, which under normal use would give them two weeks life, assuming no vegetable functioning. About three quarters of the garden was now blighted, the dehydration had stopped the process spreading any further, but they were still using up oxygen that wasn't being replenished.

At night they slept fitfully. She dreamed of suffocating, pressed into the swamp by giant fungi that had human eyes and hands that tiptoed over her horrified flesh. He lay awake in the purple dark and gazed vacantly at the apparitions of men and women that besieged him and his wife. He recognised the red-haired man and others who grinned at him lasciviously and collusively. He saw himself protesting, shouting, being held down while harpies and demons raped and soiled their bodies. In the morning they looked at each other for a moment with hatred before the need for survival rebuilt their alliance for the day.

They cleaned up the mess and replanted. Then they turned the taps on again. They took anti-G drugs which slowed their metabolism, took to their beds and prayed. If the plants grew, oxygen production would increase to the point where it would take over from the reserve supply. If the plants failed, they would have the option of dying in a desert or a swamp.

Lying in bed, they felt the lassitude and sense of unreality that every post-fever patient suffers. They felt neither anger nor fear. They barely talked. They drank water from the reservoir at their bedside. They ate a little bread and swallowed vitamin tablets. They dared not inspect the garden, some superstition held them back. They sniffed the air cautiously as the humidity came up again. The bad smell returned, worsened, improved, worsened again, improved. They were now so weak they couldn't tell anymore. They reckoned they were dying and wept in each other's arms. It was getting harder to breathe and they guessed that the emergency oxygen tanks were empty.

The decision had been made for them. Like all the others who had never returned their ship would be their tomb. Flying through the universe at ¼c there could be a good chance that their vehicle might avoid falling into some distant star and be picked up by the members of some galactic species, who would puzzle over their language and technology. They comforted themselves with such thoughts.

When they couldn't breathe anymore they would take an overdose of the anti-G drugs and go quickly and peacefully.

One evening they were surprised to find that they were no longer panting. They breathed slowly and with difficulty but the air smelled sweet, cool and moist. It smelled of the forest. They staggered out of the house and into the garden. Never before had they been aware of how silent the spaceship was. As far as they could see the garden was green and lustrous. The new plants, shining in a kind of emerald light, stood sturdily like creatures caught in a moment of dreamy reflection. Out here the air was heavy with oxygen and they breathed freely. Their world was undamaged.

PART 2

Chapter 10

They moved slowly through the bushes collecting fruit, berries and nuts. Occasionally they would scrabble in the soft Earth and pick out a potato or similar tuber. They were both naked. It was hot and they were tired but they felt no anxiety. They hadn't for over a year now. Their hair was long though carefully combed and he was bearded. There were grey streaks in his beard and in his hair. Their bodies were lean and darkly tanned. In the gloom cast by the thick sub-tropical leaves their eyes flashed intermittently like jewels. There was a riot of yellow and scarlet flowers in this area of the wood. Bees flitted from flower to flower their incessant electric hum giving depth to the space around them. They were the only insects, the only other animals on board the ship. They provided honey and they fertilised the plants. The air was humid and water-droplets condensed on the surface of the huge plexiglass dome. A pool of water had magically appeared with a tiny stream that ran into another pool. They drank from the first pool and swam in the second. They had stopped cultivating things. The "forest" seemed much larger than the garden had been, seemed to be getting larger all the time. Certainly it was changing all the time. They often got lost.

They checked the power systems periodically and spent the usual two or three hours each day navigating. They hardly talked to each other. There was little to talk about. They played games like hide and seek.

The games were often very enjoyable. They still used contraceptives, but he had stopped smoking.

At night they slept in the forest between two blankets in a hollow filled with dead leaves. The forest was dense, there were many places you couldn't see the stars at night, just green canopies of foliage, lit by the Chinese lanterns that still glowed in the dark twenty or thirty metres below. And at night there wasn't a sound except the faint rustle of leaves and the dripping of water. And all so reassuring, so peaceful.

He looked at her lying beside him in the dark. Her hair was long and lustrous, the green light picking out the purple tints. Her skin was tawny, warm and soft, a beautiful hide. He touched a nipple softly, she sighed with pleasure, stretching out over the blanket, brown leaves entangled in her hair. Sapphire-dark eyes stared into his with feline steadiness.

He heard a faint, distant gurgle from the steam that joined the two pools. It was like someone swallowing. The whole wood seemed alive. He hoped that the forest spirits had accompanied them from Earth.

Her lips, plump and soft, were parted slightly over white, pearly teeth. They glinted in the shadow. There was something indescribably savage about her. He kissed her and her body brushed liquid and sweet against his. Her open mouth closed on the tender boundary between shoulder and breast and his body quivered as her hands, birds wings, fluttered about his loins, making him sigh and ache and rise towards her. He felt another mouth attach itself to him, sucking, rippling, straightening, sending warm fires rolling along his spine. Her arms tightened about his neck, her heels ground spasmodically into his back. They were sinking into the ground, her breath harsh and hot, barbaric in his ear whispered things he could not fathom, her hips in his hands immense, opening, the throbbing going on and on. His arms tightened around her as he kissed her throat in tender passion.

They lay on their backs and looked up at the roof of leaves spread above them. The forest was an autonomous fragment of nature flying through space. Their garden was wild, was free of them. They could hide in the forest, bury themselves in the dark loam. Earth was Earth.

"What are you thinking?"

She did not reply immediately to this question and when finally she did it was with the short, unsatisfactory – "Ah, thinking!". She turned her face and smiled at him. He had never seen a woman look so beautiful. Sometimes she caused him to feel exquisite agonies. For so many years he had been resisting her. Now that she was naked her scent was headier, her skin silkier. He no longer thought of time. When she was close to him, he felt perfect. He could feel that he was falling into sleep. He smiled.

When he awoke she was leaning over him, her hair brushing his face. She kissed his eyes, the corners of his eyes, his cheek, his mouth, chin, mouth, corner of mouth.

"Do you want to …"

Her fingers traced lines along his torso, nails teased rigid penis. She straddled him, lowered herself smoothly on to him.

"… fuck?"

He sighed.

"I love you."

With snake-like movements she was pulling him higher up into her. She spoke in low guttural tones. Her twists and turns took him to the very door.

"I ... love ... you ... too. I love ... to make you ... to make you ...!"

So easy, it was so easy.

She kissed him softly.

"That's right."

Later when they bathed in the lower pool she embraced him as they stood up to their shoulders in water, her flesh warm through the cold water. Starlight glinted on the dark surface, dancing as the water rippled. Their eyes were as dark as the water, catching the lantern light as yellow stars. Stars above, below, in each other's eyes. It was a starry night, like every night, like every moment because for the rest of their lives they would always see the stars unless they found Esther's moon and hid in its mists.

He looked at her head, severed and macabre on the black lacquer. He glided towards her and kissed her mouth, barely disturbing the lacquer. The silence was black like the water. He whispered to his wife.

"Are we mad?"

Words floated among the stars.

"Of course."

Her eyes were triumphant.

They rose out of the pool and walked among the trees, letting the slight breeze dry their bodies. It was a purely vegetable world - the bees slept at night – and yet picking their way through the twisting trunks of the trees they were reminded, they both had had the experience, of childhood memories of trees as creatures that thought, whispered and called to one another.

"Aren't they beautiful?"

She was caressing a small fir tree, rubbing her breasts and thighs and belly against its rough aromatic bark. He pressed himself against her, kissing her neck, her hair, her lips as she turned her face. He caressed her slowly with his hands.

"Oh, lovely."

"You like that?"

"Oh, yes."

Presently, he found that she was weeping. She told him that she was reminded of her childhood. She whispered to the tree, incoherently but passionately, begging for forgiveness, weeping again. She would not be moved from the trunk, but clung to it as if it were her doll or a child.

Then he pulled her off the tree, and, despite her struggles, kissed her fiercely. He held her against the trunk, kissing her the while, until she began to respond to him. They calmed down and rested in each other's arms. She let her head fall back against the tree and gazed up at the stars once more. Tears filled her eyes.

"This is a dream."

"No."

They wandered back to the house. It was only visible when they were very close to it. The control center soared above it. It looked like a deserted beach house, swallowed up by the jungle. Inside however, it was still neat and airy. They used it like holiday-makers used a beach house. It was useful to cook in and sometimes they would read there, but they slept outside most nights. It was just an old beach house.

Chapter 11

If the house was strange, this was stranger. The house was now an antechamber to the magical center of their world – the control room. The screens cast orange, mauve, green and red light on their dark flesh as they walked past; they flickered like forest spirits. Some intelligent force seemed to have taken hold of the ship; the lights flashed and sparkled, numbers rippled on the screens, soft humming sounds announced that computed navigational adjustments had been effected, everything was perfect. The big machine was running perfectly. The system had matured.

They stepped lightly, they glided through this enchanting world of light and sound; they did not want to disturb anything.

In this colourful dark, they felt redundant but playful, too, as if they were tiny insects in this huge chamber, like flies that could hatch, live and die within a deserted house, living off the crumbs of ancient banquets, unseen, buzzing incessantly against the window-pane, unheard.

Their hands caressed the controls as they passed, but did not press or turn. They felt that in that way they would receive something of the magic of the machine. As they stood, naked side warming naked side, arms entwined, they felt the satisfaction of being animal.

Statuesque and entranced, they stood listening. They had undergone a metamorphosis. They were sensing the sensors, attending to the electronic systems as if they were metabolic beings. Information could be latent in a machine, unavailable until the machine had been instructed to release it. But the coded energy of the binary computer had its own peculiar harmonics, could transmit its own secret messages. She sensed it first and pulled him over towards the scanner, then he nodded and smiled. It was an emanation felt at the junction of the neck and the head. But quite clear. She smiled in return.

"Everything is energy."

She touched a button and the rear-view scan came up. Another button and the little white dot spiralled its fine line out from the center of the screen. The dot was a quarter the way across the circular screen before the first red light came on. The dot went out at Magnification 6 which was comparatively close. A couple of light years. She flicked back to Mag 5 and examined the screen. She could see nothing around the dot. She touched another button which brought in a different filter. Nothing. She began to mutter. Her husband watched the screen. His nostrils were dilated and his hands shook a little. She smelled his body change and looked at him curiously. He motioned for her to c

ontinue. She set off Computer Enhance. A misty blue light came over the screen, then yellow and finally, green. Nothing. She flicked all the way to Max Enhance and the characteristic pebbly pattern came up. This was the effect of the background radiation of the universe, the supposed remnants of the primal cosmic explosion. The red light was still on.

"There's absolutely nothing there."

Her husband demurred.

"There's got to be."

The red light went out.

"Fault."

"I don't believe it. Fault analysis."

She pressed a large black button. There was a pause, then "No fault" shone repeatedly in the middle of the screen. She pressed the button again and the flashing stopped. She sensed the adrenalin surging through her husband, felt her own fear.

"It's in Sagittarius. There's M22."

"Where's the sun?"

"Miles off. Scorpio. Backing off Antares."

"Could be taking a curve trajectory. Could be using some weird warp …"

"What are you talking about?"

"Try Mag 4."

She touched the button. The red light glowed in the center of the screen.

"Enhance."

Blue went to yellow went to green. Nothing. Pebbly effect. Nothing.

Her palms felt damp. Prickles went up and down her spine. She spoke and it came out a whisper.

"It's a fault."

"Something's triggering it off."

Insight arrived.

"It's us, we're triggering it off. We're spooking it. I mean our brain waves can activate systems, both of us were trained to do that. Now it's learned to react to our fears."

He hit the steel console with his fist.

"Damn it, we beat our paranoia, we left all that behind. If we believe that the whole damn thing's worthless. You might as well turn it off for good. There's something out there and whatever it is is so fast that …"

The red light went out again. His hand slammed to his forehead.

"For chrissakes it's a fault."

Her husband's face had the rigid intensity of the hunter.

"Mag 3."

She touched the button and the red light appeared.

"That's less than a thousand billion miles. That's our backyard."

"THERE'S NOTHING THERE!"

The red light went out.

"Mag 2."

No red light.

"Is that really Mag 2. OK. Try Mag one."

No red light.

"Open screen."

No red light.

"There's nothing there. It was just a fault. Or us."

"Check fault analysis."

"No fault" flashed repeatedly. She turned off the screen.

"Something's hiding out there. He knows we're watching him. He's thrown up some kind of screen. What's the reading you have there, what's the VC?"

She gave him the direction figures. He punched buttons.

"I'm going to laser him."

"You're crazy. It's much too far. Even if you're right you're crazy, you'll just confirm that you're on to him. Just calm down."

"OK, OK. Good thinking. Let the bastard think he's creeping up on us …"

"YOU'RE CRAZY, THERE'S NOTHING THERE."

They stood glaring at each other, naked in the starlight. He felt exhausted as if he had been drugged. He felt his eyes wanting to close, sleep called. He heard his wife speaking in low, controlled tones. He appreciated her self-discipline, even if he disagreed with it, even if …

"… nothing out there. Nothing can move that fast. We have the most sensitive scanners invented by man. They can find a safety-pin a billion miles away. There's always been an ostensible phenomenon before. Objects aren't going to break every physical law known to man so as to give a pretext for the release of your aggressive instincts. We have had red lights because of computer failure."

"… and the fault has always been picked up immediately by the monitoring function …"

"True. There's some kind of breakdown and we'll check it in the morning, we're too tired and angry to do it now."

"There are six separate monitoring functions, the chances of them all going on the blink at once are astronomical. You can't just say there's "some kind of breakdown there.". I'm an engineer and I'm telling you this ship is just about the most beautifully tuned piece of complex equipment in the universe, there's something out there that triggered off the scan."

"You once said that even the most perfectly constructed system has gremlins."

"All right, all right. I agree there's nothing more to say. I still think we should check the instruments now, together."
She hesitated.

"OK."

They returned to the scanner. Switched on the spiralling white line. Got a red light. Checked it through to a gas cloud on Mag 8. Completely routine. They found another gas cloud on Mag 6. More routine. The machine was functioning normally.

They felt exhausted, ill. They were angry and depressed, each in their own way felt defeated by the other. Drowsiness came and went.

They walked back into the forest and bathed in the pool , trying to wash off the poisons of their anger. Eventually, they crawled into their bed in the undergrowth and fell asleep.

*******   *******   *******

Just before dawn Bill visited her again. He was dressed as she remembered him the day she had completed her work on the Defence Orbiting Station. As captain of the DOS he wore the three gold stripes on his dark blue uniform of a full Commander. He had been a red-haired Irish-American in his mid-thirties, a doer and a fixer. There was a magnetic aura to him and she had been immediately attracted to him. And at the same time repelled. She sensed immediately that he had no respect for her, knew immediately that to him all women were whores. He might be cheerfully affectionate, even kind, but for him there could never be anything sacred about a woman. He was very ambitious. She could smell the ambition on him. Now he leaned against a tree in his uniform, while her husband slept beside her. She remembered that she had met him about a month before she had met her husband. In her own mind, she realised, she had always compared the two men. Her husband had been a year or two younger and congenitally at the opposite pole from Bill. They would have hated and despised each other on sight. Bill had seduced her two days after he had escorted her back to Earth.

"I always told you that I would haunt you. You shouldn't be surprised to see me."

"Go away."

"Now you know you don't mean that."

He had the most charming smile, quite disarming. He pulled a pipe and pouch out of his left-hand jacket pocket, filled the pipe and lit up from a lighter he fished out of his right-hand pocket. Clouds of blue smoke billowed around him. She looked nervously at her husband. He was sleeping peacefully.

"You're millions of miles away. We'll never see each other again. What is the point of coming to see me. I wasn't so important to you on Earth. You had other girls."

"Oh, I'll chase you around the galaxy. You shouldn't underestimate yourself. You're quite something. I'll never know what you saw in him. A loser and a dreamer from way back. Nobody ever trusted him you know."

"Coming from you that's pretty good. Nobody ever trusted you either, believe me."

He sucked appreciatively on his pipe, grinning through the smoke.

"Yeah, but people always liked me, worked with me; I'm the type that makes things fun … for everyone. But I'll tell you one thing. You're wasting your life. It's all for him. It's his game, not yours."

There was a movement beside her, her husband turning in his sleep.

"Don't worry, he won't wake up."

"How do you know?"

"I have a way of knowing these things."

She knew her husband wouldn't wake up. Suddenly, she was intensely irritated with him. He was asleep to so many things. She turned her attention to Bill, who had started to speak again.

"Shall I tell you why you interested me? You never knew what you wanted, but whatever it was you wanted it badly. A man could be secure with you, whatever he did would be wrong. An intelligent man would know he had nothing to lose with you."

"You mean I'm irresponsible."

"That would be like calling you immoral. Let's say aresponsible."

"Very clever."

"Yeah, I'm pretty smart."

"You don't have very much respect for women, do you?"

"I have a lot of respect for women. They're very dangerous. I have a lot of respect for rattlesnakes and scorpions."

"So you're afraid of women?"

"I'd never get into a hole with one. I'd never be that stupid."

Her chest felt very tight, she had difficulty getting the words out.

"I want you. Does that frighten you?"

Bill grinned, waved his hand in salute and disappeared. She felt angry but calm. She felt she had understood something. She turned away from her husband, snuggled the blanket around her and went to sleep.

Chapter 12

Water started to gather at the tip of the thick, shining, dark-green leaf that hung a few inches in front of her nose. The drop swelled, became rotund, heavily pregnant with itself, sparkled for a brief moment, became hugely, grotesquely globular, slipped its moorings and fell slowly to luxuriant splashing dissolution on another leaf a foot below.

If time was measured by the speed of a drop of water falling to the ground, then time could move here with the slow languor of a gorged lion. One's body adjusted to the effects of weak gravity, one's mind never would.

A bee, apparently untroubled by the gravity, droned by, landed on a brilliant hibiscus, crawled down a long petal into the stamens of the heart of the flower, bobbed about there and as suddenly buzzed away again. Another fat water-drop swayed eerily.

Her attention was caught by what sounded ominously like the snapping of a twig. Moving very slowly inside the bush in which she had concealed herself, she turned half around so she could look back over her shoulder and gaze through a small gap in the foliage of the bush. She could see nothing.

She sniffed gently, slowly absorbing all the vegetable smells that were wafted on the humid air. She could smell her own body, sensed the menses on the skin; her period would be arriving any day now. Was there something else? Something a little more pungent and heady? Something reminiscent of the ape? She remembered a visit to the San Diego zoo with her husband shortly after they were married. She was looking for that smell now. No, she wasn't sure.

She must have been sitting in this bush for an hour. It was getting to be somewhat boring. She looked above her at the blue-tinted dome. It didn't look anything like a real sky. It had no translucency. She touched a leaf, smiled at its smoothness, caressed it again. So beautiful. Yes, it was boring not to be moving, but pleasing, too, the lazy boredom of one's childhood which could turn so quickly to excitement, so that even when one groaned "I'm bored", there was the secret thrill of unspoken, unthought-of desires.

Ah childhood! It was not just the memories that she and her husband had collected in a previous game. Memories were not to be pursued, assembled under the influence of some desperate intention. No, childhood would be present now in the smell of the linen cupboard in a holiday cottage in Cape Cod, faded upholstery and nineteenth century oak settee and sideboy. She wondered sometimes whether all the childhood times of all the children that had ever lived were not universally available in some childhood heaven that children of all the ages could inhabit, just as children through reading could transport themselves to the Arabia of the Thousand and One nights and the jungle of Kipling's Akela.

Another crack. Well, she must stop dreaming if she was to win the game. Had she been seen? In the olive light of this jungle she felt observed by a thousand eyes; the population of the spacecraft was so enhanced. She decided that she would seek a new vantage point. She was well-hidden but not in a good position to observe. So like life – you protect yourself well but all you can see is what you can see from your castle. There would be parts of the forest where her senses might be more acute than her husband's.

She looked quickly all around her and then slipped quickly from her hiding place. To her right the forest was darker and she fled into the shadows as if a demon were at her heels. But she congratulated herself that she had moved silently. Here it was so dark that she felt free to walk rather than crawl, feeling her way, sliding her hands along lianas, pushing the leaves aside with her fingers so as to make no rustle, looking around continually to confirm that nobody was behind her. Once she saw what looked like the pale flicker of skin ahead of her, but she heard nothing and saw nothing more and guessed that she was imagining things.

Then in what she judged must be one of the darkest parts of the forest she stopped. She felt tired and angry, this was turning out to be a stupid game, it could go on for hours. She wanted to call her husband, but she wasn't prepared to admit defeat. No, but she wasn't going to go wandering around anymore. She would rest and then decide what to do. There was a shallow hollow filled with leaves nearby and she burrowed into this convenient nest.

When she awoke it was night. The air was cooler. The forest was completely silent with the bees returned to their hives and now, for the first time, she heard a faint sound of running water. She smiled and felt reassured. She was near the stream.

She headed in the direction of the sound and in a moment saw lights shining through the trees. She approached more cautiously. Her husband must have left the lights on in the vicinity of the two pools. Perhaps he had left a message for her there, or perhaps it was a trap, a candle for the moth to burn its wings on.

She moved slowly from tree to tree until she caught sight of the first hanging lanterns and the black mirror of the lower pool.

Beside the pool sat a young woman. She was leaning out over the water examining her reflection on the surface. Her body was very slim and beautiful, completely firm and substantial – there was nothing strange or ghostly about it. At this moment, she placed the tip of a long index finger on the surface of the water so that her image lurched drunkenly. There was something so beautiful and so familiar about this young girl that the woman of the ship could scarcely breathe; tears started to her eyes making the sight of the young girl tremble as if the girl herself and not just her reflection in the water were the image. But as her vision cleared so did the body of the young woman regain its substantiality, and as she rose to her feet by the water's edge her watcher was moved by the grace and elegance of her smooth hips and long legs. She lifted her head so that her dark blonde hair shook heavily across her white shoulders. Suddenly she gave a quick spring and dived into the pool. There was no disturbance of the water as her body cut the surface. Nor did she reappear.

The woman of the ship did not move. Her body was shaking with an extraordinary emotion. What was so disturbing was that she knew the young woman's name. She had forgotten the name, but there was no question but that she knew it.

She walked slowly back to the control room using the lanterns to guide her way, switching them off as she left one sector and entered another. When she had reached the control room, she turned the lights on. This was the signal that the game was over. Sitting there she felt ill and defeated. She wept quietly rocking on her seat.

An hour later her husband trudged up the stairs. He looked tired and untidy, his face and body scratched here and there. He noticed his wife looked pale and that she was trembling. They did not speak for a while. Eventually she broke the silence.

"Where were you? I looked for you everywhere."

"I was up a tree. You passed below me. I could have touched you. I followed you for a while and then you disappeared."

"I disappeared?"

"Yes, you gave me the slip."

She sighed, then gave her husband a little smile.

"You look tired."

"Do I?"

"Yes. You look very tired."

"How about you? Are you OK?"

She didn't reply. Then.

"Playing games makes it worse. It's like watching a video or movie from Earth, it's depressing. You don't play games in Paradise. Why did we start to play this game?"

"Paradise?"

"Why did we have to start to play games? We were happy as we were."

"Sorry, you've lost me."

She began to weep again and said something incoherent. His heart jolted.

"Sorry?"

"I want to go home."

Despair nearly overcame him. She no longer believed in their enterprise. There was no simple truth anymore. There was no truth. Now, he knew, he had to be a rock, he had to comfort his wife. His lips and fingers felt numb. He knew this was the first sign of death. He went through the motions. Put his arm around her. His voice sounded strange.

"Honey, it'll take us six or seven years to get back, god knows what will happen to us in that time."

"I don't care. I want to go home. I want to be normal, to have children. I'm so sorry I should never have accepted, it was an ego thing, I was competing with you, I wanted to show you I was as brave as you, that a woman could be as brave and as *stupid* as a man. Anybody can be that kind of hero, it was like you said, you just do it. I wanted to be like that, just do it. But I can't *do it*."

A squall of sobbing racked her body, her breaths came in shuddering gasps.

"I'm over thirty now. I'm getting *old*, to hell with Einstein, I'm getting older faster and faster, not slower and slower. Don't you understand? We're in hell together, this is a lunatic asylum for two people, this isn't marriage, this is the torture chamber. WHAT THE HELL DO YOU WANT FROM ME? You could have gone by yourself. You didn't need to get married – or was it that you couldn't face it alone. You needed someone to hold your hand. Is that it, is that *it*?"

They stared at each other. Neither spoke. He backed away from her and sat in the console chair. His eyes glittered in a shadowed face. She stared back defiantly. She imagined he was about to hit her. She didn't mind that, but she wasn't going to go on.

"We're going to go on."

"You're really quite mad, aren't you? There's nothing in the universe except your obsession, is there?"

"I don't care, we're going to go on."

"Mad, quite mad. My husband the maniac."

He walked out the door, trotted down the spiral stairway and into the jungle. She sat motionless now, the tears drying on her face. Time passed.

A slight noise to her left made her start. The blonde young woman smiled at her, approached her and touched her tear-stained cheek lightly. The touch of her fingers was extraordinarily soothing. A beautiful sound filled the control room. She tried to make herself speak to the young woman. She couldn't make her mouth move. She managed to force a kind of groan through clenched teeth, and then words ripped out.

"Who … are you?"

The young woman kissed her on the cheek, and walked lightly out of the room. She tried to follow her but it was as if she had been turned into a statue. She could scarcely breathe, things went dark. Looking up she watched the ceiling float away. Somewhere, in some distant place she heard the sound of her body hitting what she supposed was the floor. The ceiling seemed to recede for ever. She tired of watching it drift away, and lost consciousness.

Chapter 13

The darkness of the forest was almost palpable, the light afforded by the lanterns obscured and intermittent. He felt his way through the darkness, hands in front of him like a blind man, catching lianas and trailing branches with his fingers. He had to force his legs to walk, his arms to move. His chest felt tight, to breathe was difficult. There was a favoured place in the forest and he was determined to get there.

Eventually, he found his tree, the apple tree that reminded him of the one he had swung from as a child in California. He sat beneath it and buried his head in his hands. Hot, burning tears seeped through his fingers, huge sobs wracked his body. He could not believe that having reached such harmony in their life and in the very workings of the vehicle that his wife should throw in the towel. Everything was going so well!

He kicked the ground with his bare heel as he had done when frustrated as a boy. Why. He kicked the ground again. This was the greatest space vehicle the world had ever seen, speeding through the galaxy at a quarter of the speed of light, a jewel of a machine, the pulse of its atomic motor as regular as an atomic clock, a blazing light in the blackness of space, a white streak in the darkness. The majesty of its progress was inseparable from its precious load, the intrusion of intelligence into nothingness, of light into darkness, of measurement into infinity. A complete living environment whose biotech balance was perfect, whose navigational systems were accurate to one square metre over a distance of ten light years, whose sensors and weapon systems operated over millions of miles. All this was now threatened by the perverse, ill-disciplined reactions of a self-indulgent young woman.

But finally of course it was his own fault. He should never have allowed her so much freedom, never have allowed the garden to have gone wild. The fact that it had succeeded so well was misleading. Their own minds had gone wild like the forest.

The planners of this mission had built in the responsibility of cultivation for a purpose. They knew that too much freedom, too little goal-directed activity, would weaken their morale in the most subtle and insidious way. They should have rebuilt the garden, not been seduced and entranced by the magic of the forest, any more than he should have been captivated by the beautiful creature his wife had become. Like Odysseus he had exchanged his Penelope for a Circe – with predictable results.

They had been playing games, screwing around. He had let everything slide away from him, slip through his fingers. His irresponsibility had been colossal. They had explained to him that the success of the mission had depended upon the construction of a future that was as immense and as complex as the vehicle that was bearing them to Esther. He had to see the years stretching ahead as clearly as the trajectory they were following across the galaxy. And in those years had to be events, and ingenuity and courage. But also the ability to communicate with his partner, to support her and offer options when everything seemed to be closing in. And in that area he knew he had been weak.

But to have behaved like that would not have been natural to him. He was too much of a chancer. Play it as it lays. Yes, his perversity no doubt had inspired hers. It had been as he thought; letting the forest go wild was his way of taking a chance, of keeping his sanity by casting his fate to the winds. But his wife was getting irritated. So let her be irritated. Naturally, she wanted to go "home".

He had made mistakes, he had let things happen. But that was not necessarily all bad. It was still possible that they would survive better with a wild forest than a tamed garden. He felt stronger, more resourceful, than a year ago. There was no question but that he wanted to go on. There were certain things he had to be consistent about.

Suddenly, he felt exhausted. He wanted desperately to sleep but knew there would be no peace in the presence of his wife. He yawned and stretched out under the apple tree. It was extraordinary how secure he felt here. He reached up and picked an apple. Just ripe. So tangy. He ate two bites and fell into a deep sleep.

Chapter 14

He returned a little after dawn. He told his wife that they would continue, that there was no question of them returning to Earth. He said this in a cold, dry tone that did not anticipate disagreement. She asked him if this were his final decision. He assured her that it was. She went into the bedroom and lay down, staring up at the ceiling. Her husband had opted for hell.

The defeated always has a subtle advantage over the conqueror – he had nothing to lose. In life one should never take prisoners, not unless you need to learn the rules of imprisonment. She wanted to tell him that previously he had had a comrade; now he had a prisoner, he was holding her captive. She could embrace misery, make it her closest companion, her husband could never do that. He wanted to be happy.

She turned her head and studied the leaves on the bedroom floor. The windows had been open and they had drifted in. The house was a mess.

She had not been unconscious for long after she had seen the image of the young woman. She had got to her feet and drunk a pint of water. She had been very thirsty. She wondered at these hallucinations, the thing on the screen, the young woman. She had got to the point where she couldn't struggle with the possible significance of these non-events.

She realised that her husband was hooked on danger, he had to take a chance every day. If he didn't put himself on the line he began to fall apart. Every time he began to feel secure, he did something that put himself back in danger again. They had, after all, chosen him well, they knew he would thrive on the fear, on the uncertainty. She thought she had been like that, but she wasn't. She had had enough of endless anxiety. She wanted to be with other people again, she wanted to talk with women, she wanted to sleep with other men. She wanted to get married – properly – to a successful and capable man and have a family. She wanted the ordinary things that ordinary intelligent and attractive women have a right to expect. She was tired of spending her days and nights with an obsessive egomaniac, however fascinating the phenomenon of her husband might be.

It seemed that they had tried every possible strategy to make their life together on board ship interesting and fruitful. She thought that they had gotten very close with their jungle experience, what she called the Adam and Eve bit. Their survival after the apparent collapse of their eco-system had been practically miraculous, it had encouraged them to think that primitivism had been the answer. Well, the consequence of that was that she was seeing forest spirits, naked young women who had problems communicating. She hadn't realised that dreamland could be so exhausting. She wondered why she was so angry at the appearance of the young woman. The effect of seeing all these apparitions was simply to make her irritable.

She loved her husband, she wanted him, and yet he always succeeded in driving her crazy. If they had stayed on Earth it would have been the same. He was strong-willed, he wouldn't give in, he was a headstrong child, a perpetual adolescent, he wouldn't knuckle under like other men she had known. What she really wanted was a divorce. Well, there was no divorce here.

To obtain a divorce it was necessary that she turn this monster of a space-ship through 180 degrees and turn back for Earth. To achieve this aim she would have to incapacitate or murder her husband, literally imprison him or persuade him that they would only find happiness on

Earth. And leave him when they had returned. She assumed that her husband had also worked out the practical consequences of her animosity towards him and would be on his guard. For the moment she would have to pretend to give in gracefully to him, bide her time and wait for the right opportunity to present itself. She was confident that she would not have to wait too long.

She got off the unmade bed – they hadn't slept in it together since they had nearly died in it over a year before – and went into the kitchen. She heard her husband moving about upstairs in the control room. She made herself coffee and sat down at the kitchen table. She felt exhausted but she was not ready for sleep. She was tired of extraordinary events. She wanted merely to be ordinary, to sit at an ordinary wooden table and drink an ordinary cup of black coffee. She had no particular opinions about anything, nor did she regard herself as having any interesting thoughts concerning the past, present or future.

She heard her husband's feet clump down the stairway. They did not address each other when he entered the kitchen. He picked up a book from the settee and began to read. She looked at him coolly. It was intriguing to realise that she didn't hate him, that he was really an object for examination. As always when she had this perception of him she was stirred sexually. She knew that by her movements, by the choice of her clothes she could torture her husband to an exquisite degree; she would be torturing herself as well of course, but it was a kind of anguish that her spirit would thrive on although her face might become drawn with the strain. It would give her spirit a purpose and a goal, it would feed on the red flesh of unrequited desire. She wondered if she could push him to the point of rape. It was a challenge.

She sipped her coffee and watched him read. It was strange to consciously choose to be a bitch. She was almost grateful to her husband for giving her the pretext for it. Imagine living an entire life and never being afforded the opportunity to explore one's cruelty; she experienced a sense of relief. Perhaps that was what in his heart of hearts he wanted her to be, so that he could release his own hatred.

Her thoughts moved more easily, they were more relaxed, more juiced. She felt great power, forces she didn't understand coursed through her body, she could bend his will to her own. Inexorably, she could turn him round – and with him the ship.

Yes, there was something grotesque about this nakedness, this pretence at naturalness. Now, especially, she wanted to reserve herself. It would be strange to wear clothes again, but clothes were a crucial part of her armory.

She put down her empty coffee cup, stood up and walked back through the bedroom and into the adjoining bathroom. She turned on the hot tap of the bath. There was a short delay, a hoarse choking sound, a dribble of rusty water, and finally a burst of steam heralded spitting, gushing hot water. In three minutes she was stretched out in the bath, soaping herself ecstatically. Afterwards, she made up carefully, albeit a little awkwardly, slipped on ultra-brief panties, blue jeans and a matching navy-blue sweater. The tautness of the jeans and looseness of the sweater were the first intimations of the captivating power of clothes, the magic they could work. She brushed her coarse, black hair vigorously and studied her intense healthy face. She opened a pack of cigarettes that her husband had left neglected by the bed and concentrated on being seductive.

Seductiveness, she thought, was not merely a matter of sexy clothes. It was an attitude of mind, which was based on the understanding that every surface of the clothed or unclothed body was erotic, that every movement however apparently spontaneous was in fact deliberately tantalising. Every action, every word spoken would be set in the context of a sensual and shimmering cage of sex. She would encourage him to believe that he could take her or leave her; in reality, she would create a cosmos of seduction where each taking would lead in the imagination of her husband to ever more exotic and richly appointing takings. Her two most powerful weapons in this armory of seduction were the two languages of words and form. And the more he resisted her, the more he would whet his own appetite – and hers, of course. Her husband had a propensity to idolatry, his enthusiasm for this very spaceship revealed that. Henceforth, she must be his idol. She gave one final flick to her hair and walked slowly through into the kitchen.

Chapter 15

He was alone. He wondered at how it had come about so quickly. One moment you are communicating with someone with the ease and trust that is the fruit of seven or eight years of living together, of sharing the happy times and the bad times, the next one is dealing with a stranger. It is a stranger that he has met before; when he first asked her to accompany him on the first inter-stellar voyage, in the subsequent fantasies or premonitions of her infidelity, in the environmental crisis of the previous year. Sometimes when they made love it was the stranger he sought, the stranger in himself, too, with the implied relief from the bounds of one's moral and ethical identity. Perhaps an essential part of the erotic contract of most couples was that it should include a convention of anonymity. But in every relationship there was potentially a point of no return, where the trust could never be recreated. The trust or the respect.

That point had been passed. She had betrayed him. He could no longer rely on her. Their goals henceforth were different. She wanted to go back, he wanted to go on. She would see the continuation of the voyage as tantamount to her death; life would have no meaning en route to Esther. And a person threatened with death has the laws of natural justice on his side. He has the right to defend himself. So his wife would defend herself. As now he had to defend himself. That was the logic of war. Theoretically, his wife could fly the ship back to Earth as he could fly it on to Esther. Whether he would see such a conclusion as desirable was another matter. His wife's last words to him still burned in his ears. Would he have undertaken this trip alone? He did not know.

Effectively, his wife was now telling him that he would have to go it alone or turn back. If he turned back she would know (at least in her own mind) that her husband was chicken. She was calling him. Well, he thought grimly, she would find that he wasn't a coward.

He took a few steps across the floor of the control room. She had called him a madman. He didn't feel like a madman, but then perhaps the mad regarded themselves as sane. In fact, there was probably no doubt that they did regard themselves as sane. So investigation of one's own sanity was somewhat problematic. Sanity, for him, was a question of intentions and consequences. They had decided, freely, to fly to the nearest suitable star. Unless there was some overriding consideration that decision should be adhered to. It was to be expected there would be doubts and fears. But if one did not stick to one's agreements then everything, here, on Earth, anywhere in the universe would crumble to nothing. A man, or woman, was as good as his or her word. Sanity was to stick to one's word.

But he was close to despair. He wanted to run downstairs to plead with his wife, to appeal to her love for him, to remind her of the magnitude of their adventure and their responsibility, He knew it was no use. She would interpret it as weakness and argue more fiercely for return. She would try to wear him down, break his morale, so that overcome with exhaustion and despair he would give in to any of her proposals, anything for peace and quiet. He had to begin to prepare himself now for every contingency. He had to be ready for every accusation, every blandishment. For the rest of his life if necessary. It was a daunting prospect. For if he returned now, once they had touched down on Earth he could expect thirty years of life if he was lucky. He could start another life, even marry again, raise children. But if he went on with this it could be hell for ever. So there it was, did he have the guts to outface his wife. And ride to the stars.

He looked up in the direction of Eridanus. eEridani or Esther sparkled neither more nor less brightly than it did six or seven years ago. Why should it, they had barely covered ½ parsec and there were still 3 parsecs remaining. The light of Esther was nine years old as it reached their ship. If the star exploded this very second they would see nothing for nine years less $9 \times \frac{1}{4}c$, their own speed, which would be approximately 2¼ years. They would see nothing for nearly seven years. He might very well be headed for an illusion. Or there might be special laws of relativity that ensured that Man was for ever locked in a localised field of space and time that completely distorted the real distances of galactic space. Now, thinking like that *was* madness. Using the correct instruments Esther was measurably brighter; the human eye was a notoriously unreliable instrument.

But how percipient the old Platonists and the Eastern philosophers had been to see reality as an illusion, as the mere shadows of the true substance. That was exactly what the universe was, a vast illusion based on an appearance that no longer existed. If the farthermost stars suddenly reversed their courses the information wouldn't be available for countless millions of years, which was the distance in terms of time that the light would have to cover.

And in the middle of all this mystery and grandeur he and his wife were having a marital squabble, millions of miles from anyone and anything, totally incommunicado with their own species for a minimum of seven years. How right it had been that the first humans had been thrown out of Paradise, how inevitable and right it was. And after all, as Einstein had informed them, everything was relative. There was nothing especially peculiar about their situation in space, nor was there any particular reason why they shouldn't be having a squabble. Men and women were born to squabble. Here or anywhere.

He felt calmer. He always did after a while up here. He decided that he was ready to face his wife, and walked awkwardly down the steps. He felt tense and he had to force his legs to move properly.

His wife was sitting down drinking coffee. He did not give her more than a passing glance, picked up a book off the settee and began to read. He was conscious of his wife's eyes on him occasionally but did not look up. Presently, she got up and walked into the bedroom. Then he heard the bath water running. He hadn't had a bath for over a year. He thought he might take one later himself. Suddenly he realised he was very tired. He closed his eyes and drifted off to sleep. Evidently, he did not think his wife would murder him quite yet.

He awoke to find her standing before him, dressed in sweater and jeans. She looked at him steadily for a short while and then walked away giving him one further cool look over her shoulder. He noticed her jeans were very tight. He took a long deep breath. And then another.

Chapter 16

Hours passed and he read intermittently. He was tired and his mind kept wandering. He had spent an hour or two up in the control room. Once again there had been some irreducible phenomena on the rear scan. Much the same pattern as before; the thing kept disappearing. It was irritating, but he was too tired to think about it logically, let alone do anything about it. His confidence kept coming and going too. One moment everything was worked out, the next he felt completely confused and bewildered. The trouble was that the thoughts wouldn't stay fixed in his head. He would work something out, feel pleased that he had done so, and then realise with horror that he had forgotten what he was smiling about. He yawned and the page of his book swam away from him again. He dozed off and woke with a start, heart pounding. His wife was walking towards him very slowly.

She was dressed in a silk, moss-green gown, very low cut with string shoulder straps. This dress reached down below her knees but was open at the front in such a way that when she walked briskly, the tops of her stockinged thighs were exposed. She stood before him now, hands on her hips. With eyes half-closed and mouth half-open, saliva began to swell at her lips and fell from the corner of her mouth like the transparent, silken cord falling from the spider.

Her hands began to move over her large breasts, not touching at first and then lightly teasing the skin with maroon painted finger nails. His penis was hard and aching. She pulled the front of her dress apart like curtains, revealing tiny green briefs.

She bent over him so that her breasts swelled towards him until the silver thread fell cool and delicious on the shining head of his cock. She opened her mouth wide and then let her head fall forward, enclosing him. For a second he felt her heat and then she lifted her head abruptly, stood up, turned and walked out of the room. In a dream he watched his penis slowly collapse.

Twenty minutes later his wife emerged, dressed in sweater and jeans. She walked over to her husband, put a finger to his lips and kissed him. She sat down in an armchair and began to read a pornographic magazine. Where she had found it he had absolutely no idea.

*******   *******   *******

"What's the point of going on with this?"

He had been asleep, dreaming. He had been walking along a beach with a young woman probably his wife. The last remnants of the booming surf made weak sallies along the silver and charcoal sand, sucking at their bare feet. They had been walking arm in arm, her thigh moving in harmony with his. Now he felt cold and shaky, her voice had been cruel.

"With what?"

"With this insane enterprise. We were crazy to have agreed to go. Don't you miss life on Earth?"

"Of course. Very much. Terribly. As much as you like. I'd love to be back with you. But to give up now would be like the commander of an army who is half-way to victory suddenly having his men lay down their weapons. It makes no sense."

"It makes sense to me. I could understand someone who would do that. It would be a noble thing to do."

"But you won't lay down your arms. You won't accept the necessity of completing what you have started."

"What we started. When we were young and ambitious and blind. We have the right to change our minds."

She sat upright, trying to look reasonable. The make-up on her face undermined her expression. She looked like a sad clown.

"For God's sake stop torturing yourself. We're not going back. This is our home for the rest of our lives."

"Oh, it's horrible. Can't you see how horrible it is. How obscene it is, two little people riding this monstrosity. I wish we had died now. I was so pleased to be alive when we survived, our forest was so beautiful, but it's not a proper forest, it's just make-believe. Everything is make-believe."

"Make-believe or not, it's all we've got. We created it, now we have to live with it."

She jumped to her feet.

"WE DIDN'T CREATE IT. That's why you frighten me. You twist things. We didn't create this spaceship …"

"Man created it …"

"Man, man, man, are you "Man"? You sound like god almighty. How about "woman", how about a little *respect* for women?"

"I respect women."

She stood, an image of incredulity.

"You've never respected anyone."

He stood up now.

"You've never respected anyone, or honoured anyone, or loved anyone."

"Thank you."

She turned away from him. She was trembling violently. Then she whispered.

"I used to respect you so much, I used to admire you so much. You were ... so fine, so different from the others ..."

"I'm not so special."

She glared at him.

"Oh, you *say* that. You say it, but I don't trust you when you say it. Oh yes, now you believe it, but five minutes ago, or five minutes from now, you're going to nurse that evil little secret. That you're superior, that you're one of the elect, a hero, a space warrior. It's your vanity I despise. Your endless fucking vanity."

"And you don't know what the hell you want."

"I want to go home."

He gnashed his teeth, he was too angry to continue. He wanted to go wild, to slap her, beat her, humiliate her in every conceivable way. And he knew that was what she wanted him to do, it was just a different kind of seduction, they would end up fucking, on the floor, in the bed, or she would refuse him again, and this time there might be no come-back, never play the same trick twice. Either way, it would be exhausting, he would end up feeling rancid, just a little less able to deal with the next assault.

There was a level of existence in himself that was calm and harmonious. Sometimes, to get there he had to go through the psychological equivalent of walking over burning coals, but he knew if he worked hard enough at it he could do it. So he waited with clenched jaws and after a while the sense of oppression began to lift. He began to breathe more easily. His words when they came were low and resonant.

"This is our home."

In response, her entire being evoked despair. Her eyes pleaded with his, she seemed to be saying – you are killing me. What right do you have to treat me so cruelly. She was begging him to be merciful, to release her from this prison ... and turn back. It was only his pride that kept them fixed on that insanely distant star. She was appealing to his generosity. She seemed to cringe before his gaze. He had the moral victory, she was too weak to continue, nobody would blame him for returning; on the contrary they would applaud his selflessness and courage. For the rest of my days I will be your handmaiden, your slave. Tears fell from her eyes.

He walked over and slapped her so hard she was thrown supine on the couch. Then she turned her face slowly and gave him a look of such malice that his spine shivered. His breathing was tight and hard and he could taste the blood in his throat. He lifted her head again by her hair, slapped her again and walked up the spiral stairway to the control room, leaving her silent and beautiful on the cushions.

Chapter 17

He was too on edge to sleep and he passed the time checking the ship's various monitoring systems. Whatever problems he and his wife might be having the ship was running perfectly. As he moved from task to task an almost sensual feeling ran through him. It was such a beautiful ship. Such thoughts brought on a sexual hunger which he controlled by carrying out the day's scanning. This time there were no maverick red lights, front or rear, every phenomenon was straightforward and when he had finished, sleep was just around the corner.

He walked down the stairway, considered sleeping in the bedroom even if his wife were there, decided against this and walked out into the forest.

He entered the cool, dark glades with a sense of a need satisfied. The luxury of almost literally burying oneself in the ground was so orgiastic that all his nerves seemed to be tingling in anticipation. He did not want to be found until he had slept well and so did not retire to his usual place but instead penetrated deeper into the forest. Eventually, he found a large bush and went to sleep beneath it.

*******   *******   *******

She, too, was tired. After her husband left her she went into the bedroom, took off her sweater and jeans and crawled into bed. She wrapped the bedclothes around her tightly and prayed for sleep. She felt that she was on the edge of insanity; her mind was whirling with thoughts that oscillated wildly between tenderness and vengefulness.

Suicide and murder competed for attention, the scenario of self-immolation being immediately followed by images of the tortured and dying body of her husband.

She could not sleep, and she felt lonely and miserable. In all their time on the ship this was only the second time that they had slept apart, and she had not realised how much she had come to depend on the familiarity and reassurance of her husband's presence. And this realisation irked her; to be dependent on him, on a man, was humiliating, set her teeth on edge. Only now, it seemed, was she starting to understand how deep was the antagonism between the two of them. Essentially, they had always been enemies who had disguised their mutual hostility with a camouflage of responsibility and tenderness. And she wanted it that way, that was the perverse truth. She would rather live with an enemy than a friend. It made her feel more alive. It was more of a challenge. She loved him because she could make him hate her. She loved him passionately then. But also she hated him, she wanted him dead. She could accept that seeming contradiction and she knew that he could not.

She wanted him dead but she didn't want to be alone for the seven years it would take for the ship to decelerate, turn and return to Earth. She was not confident of maintaining her sanity or, indeed, her overall health knowing that she were a murderer over such a period of time. So, if she wanted him dead, she also needed him alive.

She rubbed the left side of her face; it still hurt. She despised him for that, so petty, childish. The ultimate acknowledgement of defeat and impotence. His face had been so blank when he hit her, blank and oafish.

That was their future now. Blank. Their life here had been exhausted of interest. Every minutia of their daily life grated on her nerves with chain-dragging predictability. There was nothing of the remotest interest; because everything that was interesting was remote. Six light years remote and increasing by nearly fifty thousand miles every second. On this intriguing thought she fell asleep.

Chapter 18

The air had cooled overnight and a thick white fog infiltrated the forest. Extractors were whining, removing the excess moisture from the air. This was a periodic phenomenon, effective for toning both human and plant metabolism.

He sniffed the misty air appreciatively and looked at the vague clumps of foliage that loomed threateningly above him. He got up from the leaf-filled hollow that had been his bed for the night and stretched. He had slept well and felt better. It was a little chilly and he was tempted to return to his warm nest but decided against it. He was hungry and for once roots and berries were insufficient. He wanted an old-fashioned breakfast.

He walked back to their holiday home as he was beginning to call it and wandered into the leaf-strewn kitchen. There was no sign of his wife; evidently she was still sleeping.

He found powdered eggs and deep frozen sausages; tomatoes still grew wild in the forest. Within twenty minutes he had just finished eating when his wife came into the kitchen. She was wearing a patterned silk negligee.

She was about to walk past him but as she came alongside his chair he slid his hand between her legs and pulled her down on to his lap. She struggled a little and then responded hungrily to his kisses. They fell on the floor, she on her back. She sighed in relief, then gasped and cried to the rhythm that slowly took them across the leafy floor.

After he had climaxed he continued to keep her down, using his superior weight and strength to flatten her body against the floor. He bruised her mouth when he kissed her. In the moments when he released her lips she cursed him softly, staring at him the while with attentive blue eyes. At times their bodies were almost motionless but for a slight tremor that repelled and linked them like an electric current. They fought and did not fight, ambiguity was in every movement. There was a convulsion, a thrashing of thigh against thigh, hand locked against hand. When desire came again he entered her, turned her round like meat on a spit, and pushed her on her hands and knees into a corner of the room. Thrusting thus from behind, he held her there rubbing her back and flanks harshly as if he were currying a horse. He entangled his hands in her hair, pulling her head back so, and so, while she clenched her teeth, her face white.

He talked to her incessantly as if she were indeed a mare to be scolded and encouraged. Finally, he slapped her on the rump, in affection, in irritation, and stood up wearily. His legs shook.

He walked unsteadily out into the forest. In five minutes he was submerged in the lower pool, seeking green oblivion in its depths.

She remained huddled in the corner of the room, her eyes blank and tearless, seeking a truth that knocked dumbly at the edge of her understanding. Ah, she was almost there, it was almost upon her. Horror or ecstasy hovered in the white-walled corner of the room, a few inches from her forehead. Had she won, had she lost? But that was not what was knocking on her door.

In the lower pool, the surface of the water was vibrating with the finest of oscillations; it was invisible to him because he was submerged, seeking answers to questions he had not the wit to ask.

But the leaves of the forest shook, moved by a motionless wind, and one could perhaps talk about sound rather than mere vibration, not yet a rumble, more the sense of a profound tension, the sense of the sound you feel just before the first flash of blue lightning. Not that there was or would be, any lightning.

She just saw dust falling on her eyelashes, dust from nowhere, irritating, making her blink, the wall buzzing as if it were covered with invisible bees, for there were certainly no bees in sight.

He was watching the surface of the water now, staring fascinated at the tiny waves, peculiar corrugations in the weak gravity of the ship. They moved so slowly, yet appeared so quickly. How strange. The water was like the surface of mercury, yes, was vibrating like quicksilver.

A roar you couldn't quite hear, a lion roaring twenty miles away in the jungle; it disturbs something in your mind.

When he leaped out of the pool he ascended a clear two metres into the air water falling off him in slow motion, great swatches of silver. His naked body bounding through the forest, tearing his skin on branches and hard, shiny leaves. The noise was easily identifiable now, a bass throb that rumbled through the ship. He threw himself through the door of their home. His wife was getting to her feet, her face incredulous. With a final moan of exasperated energy he flew up the spiral staircase, throwing switches in his mind as he went. When he entered the control room the screens were already flickering. Information concerning the secondary, environmental system came up. Everything was perfectly normal. On another screen data for the operational main reactor gleamed suddenly. He stared in horror. Core temperature was approaching melt-down if it hadn't already happened. His wife entered the control room and stood breathing harshly at his side.

"Oh christ."

"Exactly."

"Can we shut it down."

"No. Expel. What's the release code. Where's the book?"

She pulled open a drawer.

"Here. Page 8. The code is 40509."

He tapped out the numbers on the console. There was the slightest delay and then four tiny secure hatches sprang open. They pushed fingers on the buttons simultaneously. They looked at the screens anxiously. His mouth was so dry he could hardly speak.

"Is expulsion effected?"

"There's no indication of ejection explosive being triggered and the core temperature's still rising."

If they were unable to eject the motor, it was liable to cause a huge nuclear explosion that would blow them and the ship into tiny radioactive fragments.

"Try again."

They pressed the buttons again. Nothing.

"The circuit wires have melted. There's only one thing to do. We'll have to set off the charges directly. That means lasers."

She shook her head.

"I don't understand."

"There's an established procedure for dealing with lead-protected motors, basically it's like laser-based brain surgery and it has to be just as accurate. Basically you set off the explosives by using the lasers."

"Has it been done before?"

"Twice. The Russians ignited a chemically powered motor when one of their ships was falling into Jupiter in the early years of the century, and we did it to seal an atmospheric leak on the outer shell about twenty years ago. It can be done, and the computer will give us the correct angle of shot for the laser. But the lasers will have to be adjusted mechanically. That means we have to put our suits on. We're going to have to go right into the middle of the ship."

"But will there be time?"

"I've no idea. We're in the dark now."

Chapter 19

Interconnecting passageways criss-crossed the body of the ship providing access for repairs and maintenance to the surveillance and weapon systems though not the main reactors that were robotically maintained sealed units. In the unlikely event of a crisis involving the main reactors, expulsion was the only answer. The ship was overpowered in the sense that four of the ten reactors could be jettisoned without seriously affecting the capability of the vessel. Acceleration and deceleration were the only occasions when all the motors were used in conjunction; evidently the combined stress of acceleration and continued power over six years had been too much for the reactor that had been maintaining their speed at $\frac{1}{4}$c. There was a very good chance that they could continue their journey without further trouble from their power sources. In the meantime the reactor had to be ejected before it 'infected' any of the other motors, either by heat or by vibration. Ejection meant access to the weapons systems, reversing them as for maintenance or repair and then firing them in the reversed position on micro-beam setting (effectively a beam with the diameter of a pinhead, effective nevertheless for igniting the chemical explosive pack sandwiched between the reactor unit and the lead hull). Any holes made in the structure of the ship by lasers on micro-beam setting would be self-sealing thus successfully inhibiting any potential loss of atmospheric pressure through leaks. Naturally, the focusing of the three or four lasers required on a single point to general sufficient energy to ignite the explosive was a delicate matter. The settings had been worked out by computer before they entered the body of the ship. They had donned pressure suits and carried oxygen, because the entire main body of the ship, all that carried the motors and weapon/surveillance systems, was unpressurized. Because of the limitations of oxygen they would have to work quickly.

The interior passageways were composed of a tunnel sufficient for a large man to crawl down with rungs set along their lengths. But there was no up and down along these immense ladders because gravity diminished and disappeared towards the center of the ship. However the passageways were well lit. Looking down the sparkling line of lights was a vertiginous experience. Not that there was any danger of falling. One might drift slowly down or up a couple of feet. No, one floated about in these tunnels. Of course, all astronauts were rigorously tested for the slightest propensity to claustrophobia. The structure of the ship was essentially solid lead – ironically one of the by-products after fission of uranium-235, with of course, plutonium. Gold was the closest cousin to all these heavy metals. There is something meaty about such elements; have you ever cut lead with a sharp knife, discovered silver flesh under the grey skin.

They moved slowly along the tunnel, each pulling a spare cylinder of oxygen behind them. They had left two more cylinders at the tunnel junction in the middle of the ship.

Yes, there was something voluptuous about traversing these tunnels through solid lead; unconsciously, each of them caressed the wall of the passageway as they swam through. Halfway down the first tunnel she realised she was bleeding inside her suit – her period had come. The tension that had existed between them was still there – she resented the fact that he had automatically taken the lead in this new crisis – but once again an exterior crisis had eased internal antagonisms. In a way she was grateful for the interruption, contrariwise she was deeply frustrated that her husband had been able to avoid, if only temporarily, the confrontation she had needed. So as she negotiated her way through the tunnel behind her husband there was an impatience to her movements – she would have scratched the side of the tunnel if she had been able.

Also, her husband kept asking her brief questions over the intercom. This was recommended practice when using oxygen under pressure; oxygen starvation was usually not noticed by the victim until too late and constant conversation was the obvious way for each to monitor the other. She felt that she was sucked along in his wake like a little child following in her father's footsteps. She knew that even to think in these terms was childish; nevertheless, that was what she was thinking. He was the father being responsible and she was the child, inadequate to the task in hand. She remembered now that she had always wanted her own father to be more responsible, not to be so easily led by her mother. Now she was reacting as her father had done, compliant and rebellious at once.

"I can see it ahead, it's only another twenty metres." Her husband's voice was calm and measured.

In a few moments they were in the laser unit housing.

"We have to raise the tungsten shields, free the cables, swivel the unit, align on internal setting for this unit which is Code Blue, lock unit, close shields. Check?"

"Check."

"OK. Let's get to work. We have … five minutes."

The controls to move the weapon were essentially for maintenance purposes and were both electrically and mechanically powered. The tungsten shields were activated by a switch which required a master key to operate, but the laser itself though operated electrically from the control center could be moved locally by two brass wheels, which were calibrated in degrees and minutes for arc and radial settings.

"Arc 28 degrees 43 minutes, radius 202 degrees 19 minutes. Check for Blue unit."

"Check positive."

"Arc set ... now. Radius set ... now."

"Roger."

"Locking now. Unit locked."

"Roger."

"OK. Closing shields now. ... Shields closed."

"Roger."

"OK. Now for Red unit. Turn around. This time you lead."

So this time it was she who was leading, but of course it meant nothing. Her husband was effectively in charge.

When they got to the central junction they checked their oxygen, found they had plenty in hand and went to the other side of the ship, where they repeated the process in reverse, this time she making the settings while her husband confirmed the readings and the procedure. By the time they had finished Red unit they were already tired and increasingly anxious. The resonance they could feel throughout the ship had increased. They were very tempted to take a chance on the two lasers being sufficient to fire the explosive, especially since they would now have to waste more time changing over to fresh oxygen cylinders when they got back to the central junction.

She could hear the strain in her husband's voice when they reached the junction. He began the struggle of taking off one of the two oxygen canisters he had on his back, the empty one. She began to do the same. She snapped off the spring fastening that connected with the bi-valved breathing apparatus, pulled off the empty cylinder, placed it in a special alcove and fitted the new cylinder. She snapped the spring fastening into place, switched over to the new cylinder, breathed two inhalations and switched back to the other cylinder which was still ¼ full. Her husband was still struggling to release the spring fastening before removing the empty cylinder. He had left his intercom on and she could hear his breathing, harsh and too fast. She motioned for him to stop struggling and let her release the catch on the fastening. He smiled and turned round offering her access to the catch.

The fastening had jammed. Try as she could, she was unable to budge it. Her husband was impatient, bordering on the hysterical.

"Come on, I don't see that it can be that stiff ... come on for chrissake."

"I'm trying. It's very stiff, it's ... difficult ... to get any ... purchase."

"Just do it. We can't afford to screw around."

He should go back to the pressurized part of the ship, she could continue by herself, she knew what to do, but she was afraid to go down that long passageway alone, afraid of something going wrong with her equipment while she was caught in a vacuum. It was irrational, she had worked with a suit when she had been fixing up systems on the orbiting stations before she had met her husband, though never alone. It was drummed into you, the buddy system, never work alone in space if you can possibly avoid it.

"It's no good, it won't move. You'll have to go topside."

"Can't you lever it?"

"I daren't, could fracture the mounting. No, you'll have to go back. I'll be all right."

There was a metallic edge to the resonance that was rumbling through the ship. God knows what was happening; there was a good chance that the unit was now permanently fused into the main body of the ship. He was still hesitating, struggling with the catch again.

"For pete's sake, you're nearly out of oxygen, I daren't risk a quick transfer on the other cylinder. Go topside. Oh please hurry."

He turned without another word and entered the tiny elevator. Within a minute he would be in the pressurized part of the ship.

She entered the tunnel to the third and final laser unit. The resonance was very bad now; several of the lights in the passage had been damaged by the vibration, so there were times when she was in almost complete darkness, apart from the small lamp set in her helmet. She pulled herself along by the rungs, uncertain how much time she had left, fearful of being unable to carry out the necessary functions. Suddenly, all the remaining lights went out, one of the fuses must have blown. All she had left was the weak illumination afforded by her personal lamp.

She stopped, overcome with panic. She felt sick and was terrified of vomiting in her suit, it was so easy to choke. She knew at least three astronauts who had died that way. Shaking all over, buffeted by the vibration from the rogue reactor, she clung whispering to the rungs of the ladder. Eventually, the buffeting eased a little, or she grew accustomed to it and she breathed deeply and slowly, and began to feel her way along the passageway again.

She practically crashed into the laser unit. Without thinking she released the switches on the shields, opened up the shields, swivelled the laser freeing the cables more by feel than sight. Sweat was pouring into her eyes as she turned the little brass wheels setting arc and radial readings; she could barely see the figures for the settings with the tiny light in her helmet; the unit maintenance lights had also fused. She prayed that the circuits carrying the power to the lasers were intact. To generate the power to fire the lasers one of the other nine main reactors would have to be started up; the chances were that the damaged reactor had ruined its associated dynamo.

She locked the unit in position, closed the shield and slid back along the tunnel. Everything was shaking and banging now, but she was no longer afraid. She expected the whole ship to go up any moment.

She was finding it extremely difficult to hold on to the ladder. She'd move along a couple of metres, be thrown back a metre. She felt like a pebble in a tube being rattled about. Panic came back again, but she kept going this time, her panic turned into frantic movement.

She was aware of a dim light to her left. Another few moments of crashing and bumping and she wriggled into the lift which had its own lighting system. The doors closed, and she was rushing towards the living quarters of the ship.

She struggled out of the pressure suit and ran up to the control room, panting desperately. Her husband was bent over the controls.

"I'm just firing up Reactor C. Green Unit OK."

"Yes."

"Switch on rear view scan. OK. Good."

There was a terrific jolt, and a palpably increased G-force.

"C's on line."

He looked at the screens that were flashing manically with every colour of the rainbow.

"We have full current from C. let's strap ourselves in. OK. I'm firing the lasers now …"

This time the shock went right through their spinal processes, there was a muffled roar …

"OH BOY, OH BOY, look at that, will you. That is beautiful, just look at that baby blow …"

Her husband was pointing up at the rear view TV screen. A morass of yellow and white molten metal and flame was receding fast behind them.

"Perfect, absolutely fucking perfect. What speed are we building up to? Not to worry we'll be back on ¼c in a couple of minutes. Wow, we were so lucky, I mean I've never seen a whole reactor go off like that … OMIGOD … OMIGOD."

The screen was a pure sunrise of pink and white light that illuminated every corner of the control room.

"That's a thousand megatons or it's nothing at all …"

She was speechless. She wanted to say nothing, to think nothing. The ship trembled as the radioactive plasma from the nuclear explosion hit and raced on through the universe like a tiny supernova. She wondered if anyone on Earth would see this tiny sign of their passage seven years from now; if they did they would assume that their mission had ended in disaster. She could not bear to think that they had been so close to death, that their hold on existence was so precarious.

The spaceship was completely silent. The monitoring screens glowed in reassuring normality; there wasn't a single sign to indicate the crisis they had just overcome.

They were both exhausted. Over the last three days their time had been so crammed with incident that any further reactions or decisions were impossible to contemplate. Her husband looked at her wearily – and warily.

"You almost certainly saved our lives by setting that last laser. The chances of the explosives being ignited by two beams were very remote …"

He hesitated.

"I don't want us to go on fighting like this …"

"Nothing's changed. I'm too tired to talk now. All that's happened over the last few hours only makes me want to go back the more. As far as I'm concerned this ship is schizophrenic. One moment everything is going perfectly smoothly, the next we're anticipating being blown to smithereens. Now I'm going to get some sleep."

She lifted herself out of the chair, stumbled down the stairway and fell into bed.

He felt dizzy and frustrated. Why had he made himself vulnerable by calling for a truce. The fact that she had saved their lives? She had only acted professionally, and she had a vested interest in his survival. She would want a companion on the journey back to Earth.

For the first time he felt close to despair. His emotional resources, his resilient optimism, seemed to have entirely drained away. He had implicitly believed that anything were possible if one were determined enough. Now he was beginning to feel that he had constructed a perfect trap for himself, that his unconscious had carefully worked out a situation which would set the opposed aspects of his character in perfectly balanced opposition. He, the engineer, had engineered the construction of a house perfectly designed to fall in on itself once the right circumstances obtained.

Yes, his paranoia had imploded on itself. He didn't require any further fantastic figures to remind him that something was wrong. He was his own enemy. So how do you defeat yourself. By returning to Earth or by continuing without conviction. Which was the greater suicide.

Or was this perfectly normal, this state of moral anxiety, the inability to make a satisfactory decision? Perhaps the design was after all perfect, that it was necessary for he and his wife to travel six or seven light years away from their own planet to confront their destiny, which is the destiny of every human being. A destiny of dissatisfaction. And from the realisation of that dissatisfaction, but only by an ultimate *realisation,* might it be possible to win the peace of acceptance. The dream of millennia.

He climbed down the stairs, got into bed beside his wife, kissed her as she slept and in a few moments was asleep himself.

PART 3

Chapter 20

The field of green wheat stretched into the distance. It rustled softly. They still had tons of flour left of their original store but that was not the point. He had needed a new challenge. He had found the seed-corn preserved in the freezer. Half of it had produced this cornucopia. Every day he went around the perimeter checking that no weeds crossed into the field. Another few weeks and the corn would begin to ripen. The wheat-heads were healthy and full. It would be a good crop. Small threshing and milling machines were part of the equipment of the ship. All the harvesting would have to be done by hand but he looked forward to that. He hoped his wife would help him; it would do them good to do something together.

He took off his check shirt and let the warm air dry the sweat off his body. He threw himself down on the low Earth bank that surrounded the field and looked up at the blue dome. He brushed his fingertips through the gritty, dusty surface of the soil. He looked at his hands. They were no longer the hands of a young man, and the recent work had made them rougher. And yet he still looked youthful. Perhaps time was slowing down as predicted. They had been travelling for seven years. It felt like three or four. He rubbed his skin in disbelief. As for his wife. Every day she seemed to become more glamorous. Her body was firm and sinuous, her skin dewy. Her eyes shone, her teeth sparkled.

She was as enigmatic as ever to him. She no longer seemed to resent him. But she still maintained that they should return to Earth. Sometimes they would make love with animal pleasure, sometimes they would scarcely exchange a word. Sometimes he suspected what she was getting up to when alone in the control room.

Beyond the field the forest was as wild as ever. Fruit and vegetables grew plentifully so there was no need to cultivate them. And they enjoyed their walks in the wood. Things had changed. They had more choice but they also realised the need to have a sufficiency of tasks. They did not approach things so directly, communication was terse, at a minimum. Even their lovemaking was almost matter of fact, perfunctory but satisfying to the spirit.

What had become clear to him was how closely their state of mind was related to the overall character of the ship. It was almost as if their craft had developed a character of its own; it seemed to tell them what its needs were. And these needs became their own needs. Slowly, they were becoming acceptable to the spaceship. That was how it seemed. The reverse of what they had anticipated.

They watched the instruments in the control center as carefully as ever. More carefully. Since the explosion an anxiety that had perhaps always been latent became evident. Their ship was not perfect. They now used their motors by rota. The ejected motor had started to tear itself apart as a result of metal fatigue. It had been overstressed.

Sometimes he found himself moving around the ship as if he were on tiptoe. He recognised that this new nervousness was a consequence of the accident and that it would pass with time. Or perhaps, despite appearances, he was getting soft.

He walked back to the house. His wife as he had anticipated was in the control tower. She was wearing a white swimsuit and a red cloche hat. She grinned as he entered the room.

"Hallo."

"Hallo."

"How is the wheat?"

"OK. A few weeds. Not too many. How are things up here?"

"Fine. Just finished the rear scan."

"Red lights?"

"A few. All present and accounted for."

"Sure?"

"Of course, I'm sure. I wouldn't lie to you. I'll make us some lunch in a minute. I'm just finishing off here. Almost done the forward scan. Looks like a plasma cloud up ahead. Quite a deep one from the configuration so we'll get some pretty lights for a while."

He walked round the chamber looking at displays.

"Motors seem OK."

"Yes, they're good."

"Fine. Well, I'll see you in the kitchen in a while."

She looked at him steadily for a second.

"OK."

He walked back down the steps. Maybe he should have offered to make lunch. Maybe he should cut his throat.

In the control tower it felt like a summer day. There was no objective reason for that. It just felt that way to her. She felt the girl had joined her today and this made her feel happy. It was good to have company. And she was so easy, so relaxing to be with.

It was not that the girl said anything. It was her presence that was so pleasing. With her husband in fact and her lover in fantasy there was always a competitive edge that she increasingly felt as a strain and a pain. The sexual arousal that Bill occasioned was exciting but exhausting. She always felt ill after he had visited her like a hangover after drinking. She had discovered that the girl was called Diana, appropriately – as a kind of forest spirit.

Diana had explained that she had come to the ship because she had heard the woman's call. That was her role, to go where she was called. That was why she was so happy. She was always wanted, The woman of the ship agreed that that must be wonderful – always to be wanted.

"Oh it is. But sometimes the person who needs me is not always aware of it. So when I arrive the person is surprised and frightened. Like you, for example."

She was standing now a few feet in front of the woman resting her hips against one of the display consoles. Blonde hair fell confusedly over her shoulders.

"But I knew you. Recognised you. That was what was so disturbing."

The girl looked at her mischievously.

"Well, I didn't recognise you. I just knew that you needed me."

"Can you explain my knowing you?"

The girl shrugged.

"Who knows? Can you explain everything in the universe? All I know is that I have to please. I want to please you. That is the most important thing."

"So you don't know where you have come from."

"I have very few memories. The clearest thing about me is my name."

"Can my husband see you?"

"Your husband never sees me. But he saw your other friend once."

"Bill?"

"The one with the red hair."

"So he knows!"

"No, but he suspects – and that is worse. For a man like your husband to suspect without proof is a kind of crucifixion. He will torment himself on his integrity, unless …!

"Unless …?"

"Unless he can defeat himself."

"I don't understand."

"You are not your husband."

A gentle chiming announced that it was twelve o'clock. When the woman looked again Diana had gone.

She was waiting on events. She had a secret and she would keep it. She had given her husband every opportunity to return to Earth. Life was a holiday – he was enjoying the waiting.

Increasingly, she saw her husband as an innocent. Since the accident she saw him differently, and although on the surface he had got his way, she felt that underneath the balance of power had tilted in her favour. He was so single-minded, all he could see was the spaceship and their trajectory towards Esther, he was unaware of all the forces that might be sending him in a different direction.

As for herself, she seemed to be poised on the pinnacle of a myriad of invisible currents that promised to send her flying in totally unforeseen directions to discover aspects of herself that had been buried under years of her husband's control. She thrilled at all the things she might be. In the meantime, she was getting hungry. There was something perversely satisfying about cooking a meal for someone you are trying to outwit.

That was the strange thing. Now that her future had been decided she found that she was actually enjoying her husband's company. Sex is always most pleasurable with the one you are about to destroy.

Chapter 21

It was dark in the bedroom. On the videoscreen Astaire and Charisse were dancing in Central Park to the slow, passionate rendition of "*Dancing in the Dark*." Tears slid down his cheeks.

Chapter 22

Outside the ship diaphanous coloured waves advanced and retreated like the spangled transparent gowns of a corps de ballet. Occasionally, in a vast electrical discharge there would be a momentary flash of blue light, quite soundless in the airless domain of space, and the beautiful cellophane gowns would be blown away momentarily before surging back in a palpitating rush.
They looked out at this drama, like two children at a window watching a thunderstorm.

"Do you miss the theater?"

"West Coast people were never very big on theater – except in the movies. If you don't see it in the cinema, it doesn't exist – it's a kind of Californian Cartesianism. Theaters are too constricting for Americans."

"I like the theater and I'm an American."

"You're from New York."

"Connecticut."

"It's all the same thing. It's still one foot in Europe. America starts at Illinois. That's when I start to breathe, when the Yankees are behind me. If I had to live anywhere in the States I'd live in Chicago. I'd be comfortable there at the center of things. Chicago has mystery. It's nothing and everything. I think I'll call this ship Chicago. Because it's the center of everything."

"We could go back and see Chicago."

"I knew you'd say that. Chicago is here. New York is here. Connecticut is here. California is here. Because we're here."

"That's crazy thinking."

"No more crazy than the English, Spanish, French, Portuguese, Dutch that created the Americas. Out of nothing – or out of everything that was missing in Europe. Now we're doing the same thing. Carrying our world with us like a snail with its house on its back. Yes, ultimately we're those same restless Europeans that could never accept defeat at the hands of Nature. Nature's gangsters. The angry children of the world."

She looked at him in wonder.

"There are times when I realise that I had no idea of who you were when I married you. I was dwelling under the misapprehension that you were a pilot or an astronaut or something. The biggest mistake I ever made."

"I am a pilot, a flyer. Saint-Exupery was a flyer. Just because you do a job like flying doesn't mean you stop thinking or seeing. It's like I said. You're just a Yankee snob."

"So why did you marry me?"

"You know why."

"Tell me anyway."

"OK. You were the most beautiful, most captivating woman I'd ever met."

"Captivating?"

"Yes, captivating."

"Is that why you had to make a captive of me? Because you couldn't stand the idea of being captured."

"This is getting pretty close."

"We could get closer."

"Yes."

They began to make love. Nature's holograms flickered outside their window. Somewhere in their depths, Astaire and Charisse strutted and whirled.

Chapter 23

There was something premonitory about the hieroglyphs. They were burned into the stone with a furious insistence. It seemed extraordinarily important that he should decipher the message. He strained his mind, seeking anything that was recognisable in the alien signs. The only thing he thought he recognised was a small winged insect, an image that was repeated later in the series.

He passed his hand over his brow in a gesture of fatigue. Everything was there in front of him if only he could read it. The intensity of the message grew as he studied it. The marks on the stone seemed to be smoking in the sun, the way leaves smoulder under a lens. He looked around him. There was only the sun, the sea and the birds, quivering, practically motionless in the stiff breeze. The air was so pure, so intoxicating, there was so much of it! A whole world of fresh, unadulterated air. And all for him! Like *Robinson Crusoe* but instead of an island, a planet.

But who had written the hieroglyphs? The marks looked fresh. In which case he was very far from being alone. Perhaps at this very moment he was being watched by hundreds of eyes. Once more, he looked around. There was nothing but the sun, the sea and the birds. But where was his wife?

He woke to see her asleep beside him. He touched her hair gently. He had forgotten how tender he could feel towards her. Why had they become enemies? Blame it on society?

Society was just another infinite series of his and hers. Nor did his dream seem to shed any light on the matter.

He had left the Earth because everyone he knew seemed to be stuck in a History that was written and updated hour by hour. Life this year was significantly or insignificantly different from life last year or life five or ten years ago. He and all his friends, such as they were, were more or less unconsciously measuring and judging themselves by standards that were always elusive because always changing. You dare not miss television or a newspaper in case you missed the definitive analysis of what was modern. Modernity was the metaphysics of the age, reflecting a self-obsession that stifled every joy at conception. Even if people claimed to be old-fashioned it was with the implicit intimation that they were old-fashioned in the very latest way. Silence was the only answer to this institutionalised narcissism, but of course people thought you were mad.

There seemed to be two choices, either to become an anarchist and destroy as much as you could or get the hell out and fly for ever. He had opted for the second because he had the means to do it. One thing was true. He had never regretted his decision. He supposed it was to do with his Californian heritage. The only way out was the big blue – or madness. He was lucky, he was part of a machine that was as monstrously large and fast as his ambition.

But he wondered whether this really was Chicago, or whether if he had moved to a different city he might not have found an authentic community. The community he could respect and play his part within. Or was he simply the type that would always try to break up every group of which he found himself a member? Was this extended voyage his way of trying to grow up, his particular version of the Grand Tour? Would the prodigal son return, only to find that no-one remembered him? He smiled. It was a condition of the lonely that they should worry about confronting a justice that was always poetic. A peculiar vanity.

In the meantime, here was he, here was his wife, and here was the ship. Here was the human condition as found in outer space.

His wife stirred beside him. Presently, he was looking at her eyes looking up at him.

"What were you thinking?"

"I was thinking that I shall be a very old prodigal son when I return."

"You're going to be such a vain old man. Only you could worry about what people will think of you as an incredibly old and probably senile case. You'll probably be completely bewildered and remember nothing. An old grinning fool."

"No, I won't be like that."

"You can't tell."

"I may be irritable, but I won't be mad."

"No-one thinks they're mad."

That was true, he had thought that. He hesitated so his wife continued.

"I've always thought you were a little mad. You always seemed to miss things that other people understood quite easily. Other people just accept things; you always had to question everything. Childish really. You just never grew up properly. Other people don't make such a fuss. They get on with life. You're always brooding. Hatching ideas like an old hen."

He stared at her.

"What the hell are you so angry about?"

"I'm not angry."

"You're angry and you're jealous. Forget other people. Speak for yourself. You resent the fact that I think for myself and act for myself, that I can take responsibility for my own actions."

"So we're back with responsibility again. Well, I think I've been pretty responsible. The thing between us is about power. The fact of the matter is that you don't trust our relationship enough to ever give in on anything important to you."

"For example?"

"For example, there's no way that you will consider turning back, however unhappy you make me. You'd drive me to distraction but you'd never give up on that, would you? There's going to be no consensus, just a battle that will get worse and worse. What is the point of my being here? I'm wasting my life, I've a future to look forward to that will be a living hell, and you're prepared to put me through that for the rest of my life."

"I hope you'll change your mind."

"There's no way I'm going to change my mind."

"Then live with the consequences."

His heart was beating wildly, he wanted to strike her dead. There was a look in her eyes that was triumphant and truculent at once. Again, he felt that she wanted him to hit her. He so wanted to oblige; the madness bubbled in his brain, choking his thoughts, his calm, his aspirations for happiness.

"We both have to live with the consequences."

He didn't reply, there was nothing to say. This had been the pattern for nearly a year now. You think things are getting better, you are making what appear to be the right changes, you sense progress, that life is being enhanced, that positive things are being done – and then this corroding frustration, this mind-numbing resentment and hatred, this disgust. And everything has to start all over.

"I suppose you want to go for a walk and a sulk. Go and beat the bounds of your little kingdom."

He remembered the family garden, walking around the fence at daybreak to see if any rabbits had tunnelled under the wire mesh. The huge pink roses with the dew on them. The smell of fresh coffee from the kitchen window. The old motorcycle that he was rebuilding, a vintage vehicle, an English Triumph. Beautiful and gone for ever.

"You've got to have a little faith. You can't go back, you've got to go on. Something will happen, something you would never have expected."

"You and Mr Micawber. That's pathetic. Nothing happens unless you make it happen."

"That's only partly true. I used to think that was the whole truth. Now I know it's not. There is the unknown and your relationship with it is the most important thing in life. What lies beyond your own will. That is the most important thing."

"Well, I'm tired of all that transcendent rubbish. It's just a con trick. It developed, all religions developed, to make the insufferable sufferable. But even if I went along with you I'd have to say that we had no business leaving life on Earth. Life is sacred, and human life most of all for most religions, so even on that basis we have no right cutting ourselves off from it."

"We're not cutting ourselves off from human life. We're devoting our lives to finding another world so that human life may prosper in some other part of the universe. In a way we're sacrificing our own lives so that future generations may live."

She stared at him in incredulity.

"I can't believe I'm hearing this. I just don't believe it. I can't believe you've become so hypocritical, and so sanctimonious. You *hated* life on Earth. You couldn't wait to get away. This trip was heaven-sent for you. Heaven-sent. It was *perfect* that you were the one that was chosen. You always thought I didn't know that, but of course I knew. Everybody knew. All that fake emotion about leaving your friends but of course you weren't *really* leaving them because you would be carrying them in your heart. You've never given a moment's thought to any one of your so-called friends since we took this trip. Well, let me assure you it was a two-way street, plenty of people gave a sigh of relief when you went up in the air."

He gnashed his teeth and went into the kitchen to make coffee. The feeling he had in his dream, the frustration at not understanding something was still with him. He always had the sensation when he and his wife were arguing that the real subject of the argument was elsewhere. That was the true frustration, the sense that you were very close to the answer and yet it always managed to evade you. If you choose the right direction in life you quickly make the right connections, but if you make the slightest mistake you end up on a trajectory that will take you through the emptiness of isolation for ever. Was that what had happened to him, perhaps to his wife too, that at some point in their lives, perhaps at twelve or seventeen or twenty-three they had made a decision that had had irrevocable consequences? It was not the accusation of hypocrisy that upset him, it was the implication that he didn't know what he was doing that he was out of control. In principle he was correct; it was evidently admirable that they should devote their lives to finding a haven for humanity. But could an expedition that was characterised by hatred bring anything but misery to those who were to enjoy the fruits of its success – assuming they were successful. On that basis every cross word that he and his wife exchanged represented somebody's death. He shivered. That way madness lay.

The feeling of oppression grew. There was something in the air. He was picking up something. Whatever it was was disturbing. He watched the coffee percolating as if it were a hot spring captured by a silver cylinder. There was a message he wasn't reading correctly. Things in the ship had changed. He had put it down to the methods of cultivation, but it was something else. He closed his eyes. He tried once more to see the hieroglyphs. They refused to materialise, but there was no feeling of frustration; his anxiety had gone. It was his wife. Her attitude towards the situation, to him and the future had changed. She was irritable but she was no longer desperate. She was therefore confident. And she wasn't acting, the confidence was real. She knew something.

He poured out coffee into two mugs added milk and sugar to one and walked thoughtfully back into the bedroom. He handed his wife her coffee and sat on the edge of the bed. The silence deepened a little. He cleared his throat. The silence deepened a little more.

"I thought I'd do the navigation today. Make a change."

She looked puzzled.

"OK. I take it you see no further point in continuing our discussion."

"That's right. Anything I should look out for on the screens?"

"What kind of things?"

"Anything unusual."

"No, there's been nothing."

"Fine.

He showered, shaved, dressed and went up to the control room. Later he watched her walk into the garden. She didn't look up but then these days she never did. But her walk was very expressive. She looked stiff and ill at ease. He touched buttons and the screens began to hum. She was no longer wearing her swimsuit and hat. She was back in sweater and jeans.

Chapter 24

He had found it almost immediately on the rear scan. Computer enhanced visual denoted a circular craft travelling at about ¼c. Records showed that his wife had picked up signs of the alien ship nearly four months before. The pattern was sketchy however because the progress of the ship had been so erratic. At times the computer had estimated its speed as anything between ¼ and 1½c. It had kept appearing and disappearing and appearing again in unexpected places, making it very difficult to differentiate it from any random clouds or debris. When it broke light speed it simply presented no profile, it literally disappeared. It darted around like a mosquito. It was an extraordinary accomplishment that his wife had managed to track it at all. He had first noted the phenomenon of the object that caused the red dot to come on and off nearly a year before; evidently it had disguised its presence for a further six months or so. Or perhaps this was a different vehicle. If so it was of the same type because the pattern of its behaviour was identical to what they had originally observed. Now the other ship was approximately 30,000 million miles away, perhaps as little as two days behind them – or less. It had been in that position for a week; perhaps its commander had decided to see if he could provoke a move.

But why had his wife said nothing? Realisation dawned as soon as he had asked himself the question. She was gambling that the ship was friendly and could rescue her from her cage. That was not unreasonable; American technology had been easily superior to that of any other country and the possibilities of it being an extra-terrestrial vehicle were remote in the extreme. There never had been any sign of alien ships in solar or deep space. Correction: there had been signs but all had proved to be pseudo-phenomena.

And was this, too, a pseudo-phenomenon? The computer thought not. It had a very specific profile, both of form and behavior. It was astonishingly fast and one had to assume that it carried a repertoire of capabilities in terms of performance and weaponry that superseded those of his own ship. His own weapons were only effective over millions and tens of millions of miles, distances that would be estimated in light seconds or a light minute or two. Even at 2c the other ship was still days away and it seemed likely that 2c was dash speed. So what was it doing there?

He felt profoundly depressed. He had been alone, the first protagonist of his solar system to venture out into deep space and traverse it. Now he understood his wife's sneer about inspecting his little kingdom; enjoy it while it lasts was the hidden intimation.

He smiled. Of course it was typical that he had assumed that the other ship was antagonistic to him. The chances were that he knew several of the people on it, as would his wife. The other commander was being tactful, giving him a chance to get used to the idea that a way of life that had obtained for over seven years had come to an end. The correct response was to cut his motor when he was ready and allow the other ship to make contact. That was the established procedure. And yet the way that the other ship had come up to them, the darting about all over space, the clear evidence of camouflage and disguise implied the aggressive profile of the stalker. This joker was giving out a very ambiguous message. And his wife said nothing.

For him to follow suit, to throw up a radio-plasma screen, to activate LMI and play his own disappearing trick would confirm that he had moved to battle station and in any case was premature; the potential enemy was much too distant. There was also the enemy within. What was he to do with his wife? Tie her up and throw her in a cage. He didn't have a cage. There weren't even any locks on the door. But there was a procedure in case of insanity. A paralysing pellet followed by a strait-jacket. But the other commander would expect a more or less happily married couple – anything else would arouse his suspicions. No, he had to use his wife's eagerness to establish links with the other craft to his advantage. His wife had to be the staked goat. And he? He had to appear to be harmless, even compromised.

In the meantime his wife expected him to find the intruder in what they had comfortably regarded as their own space.

He doubted that he could pretend not to have noticed anything on the scan; his wife was very sensitive to his moods and perceptions and in any case was expecting a reaction from him. He was going to have to acknowledge the existence of the other vehicle at some point – it might as well be now. His actions now would be crucial both in terms of the reactions of the other commander and of his wife. He switched on the intercom.

"Emergency. This is an emergency. Come to control."

In less than a minute he saw his wife running towards the house. He heard her panting as she went up the stairs.

"What's the matter?"

He spoke savagely.

"You know what the matter is. Look at this. What the hell do you mean by not telling me?"

"I was going to tell you. I wasn't sure, I wanted to wait until I was sure. We went through this before – it was all speculative."

"Have you thought of what the consequences of this could be. It's almost certain to be an American ship. He's shown us that he's very quick indeed, now he's following connection procedure; he's been maintaining station for a week, he's been giving us a chance to get used to the idea. You should have told me that."

"Well, I'm sorry. What should we do now?"

"We have to cut our speed. He should catch up and then identify himself when he's within a million miles or so. We'll have to be ready for anything before then."

"How do you feel about it?"

"I don't know, it's too early. I don't want to talk about it. You don't tell me anything for months and then you ask me how I feel about things. We'll talk about it later."

"OK. So what do we do now?"

"We prepare for deceleration. Once he sees we're slowing he'll be with us almost instantly – in a day or two. We'll know immediately he accelerates because he'll just disappear."

"As he goes through light speed."

"Yes. The computer has estimated his fastest speed as $1\frac{1}{2}c$ - it could be 2, it could be 3, who knows? With a ship like that interstellar travel becomes a practicality. In comparison, we're just crawling across space. I don't even want to think about it. We're superseded, let's leave it like that for a while. OK, we're going to have to be strapped in. I suggest you make some sandwiches or something. Formally, we enter battle stations as of now, so we get into our suits. We'll need 24 hours supply of oxygen. That should be enough. Of course this conversation is being recorded as will every aspect of what we say and decide from here on in. Is everything stashed down throughout the ship?"

"I would say so. I'll get some food, water and the suits. When do we start to decelerate?"

"Soon. About an hour. At 1100 hours. That should give us enough time."

He watched his wife walk down the spiral stairway. While she was gone he spoke hurriedly but quietly into the microphone, recording for whoever might be listening his analysis of the situation and some of his more general intentions. Then he went through a check list of all the ancillary functions he would be calling on over the next hours and days. He checked his field force generators and the weapons. His passive and active defence systems. He started up two of his atomic motors; these would provide the power for the systems. Lasers hummed. He closed the motors down again. They donned suits and established that everything was at hand. They turned off all lights throughout the ship so that the only illumination came from the soft glow of the VDUs and the blue lanterns of the battle lamps. There was a whine as the control nodule turned through 180°. Then the ship went completely silent and they were gently pushed into their seats. He pressed a switch and the rear view scan came up. The visual information of their manoeuvre sped towards the circular mark on the screen at 186,000 miles every second. Theoretically, it should take two or three days for the alien ship to receive that information over the tens of thousands of millions of miles distance. Ten minutes after they had cut their motor drive the other ship disappeared. They looked at each other through their visors. His wife whispered over the RT.

"I'm frightened."

Chapter 25

Now she was not so sure. She had anticipated the possibility of the present scenario but it had not been her first choice, though she now had to admit that it had always been the most likely one, despite the fact her husband had taken so little interest in things navigational since last year's crisis. He had become obsessed with the smooth running of the ship. And now at the crucial moment this sudden change.

Once again she had to acknowledge the almost uncanny sense of survival that brought her husband back from the brink, that alerted him to danger. The girl had warned her that her husband had "seen" Bill. Did he know now, as she did, that Bill was the commander of the ship that was pursuing them? They had been meeting every night after her husband was asleep. As soon as her husband had made the decision to slow down she had warned Bill, and immediately Bill had given the order to go to max speed. Was her husband beginning to listen in? Yes, she was beginning, for the first time, to be a little frightened. It was not unpleasurable this feeling of fear and for the first time in a long time she looked at her husband with curiosity.

The silence of the ship was strange; for seven years now they had been powering through the universe, the distant throb of the motors had become as familiar as their own heartbeats and as unheard – until they stopped. In the semi-darkness a bee was buzzing somewhere. It buzzed for a while then stopped, buzzed again and stopped. She lay on her back and gazed sightlessly at the screens.

Her husband was lying beside her. She tried to tune into his thoughts but couldn't; it was ironic she could talk with a man millions of miles away while the man beside her was impenetrable. She could make out his features under the raised visor – somber, a masked face. Every minute or so the mask blinked. The light from the screens glinted occasionally on his eyes.

What would her husband do? His ship was obsolete, he would have to bow before the force of superior technology, he respected that above everything. The other ship was American, he would respect that too. There would be nothing for it but to give in gracefully, acknowledge the absorption of their mission into that of the superior ship. Because she knew that Bill too was on the way to Esther.

The other ship would be with them in less than 24 hours. Her husband had guessed pretty accurately. 2c was about the speed that the other vehicle would be making. She knew that because Bill had told her.

Everything had changed. They could reach Esther in four years, there were other men and women on the ship, the crew's complement was about a hundred. The ship was huge. Mysterious and magnificent. They would be back on Earth in ten years; it was an adventure that no sane person could refuse; the opposite of their own mission which no sane person should have accepted.

She was reminded of the hours before launch. The solitude after months of training, programming, confronting friends and journalists. And then the hours before the final lift-off, the lox being fed into the huge booster rockets that could take their craft out of the atmosphere, the myriad checks on all aspects of their vehicle. And then the silence, looking at the brilliant sun in the blue sky; such a beautiful day, she remembered she cried, the tears streaming under her visor, such a confusion of emotions, pride, much love for her husband, anguish that she would never see the Earth again in all likelihood, and then the strange, almost tangible pressure of her training, gently lifting her away from the past and into the mysterious future, soothing her desperate body with the promise of the unknown, and then almost before she was ready for it, the mind-shattering roar of the boosters, and then incredible pressure, a torture that threatened to go on for ever and drive her spirit from her body. Her last memory of life on Earth being her husband grinning at her, an image that was reassuring and terrifying at once. He was enjoying it!

This was so different. They were so different. Her husband wasn't grinning now. She preferred him this way. But she still had no idea what he would do.

"What are you going to do?"

The silence deepened. After a while she began to wonder if he had heard her. The mask beside her showed no emotion. It blinked at the same rate. It stared at the screens as if hypnotised. His voice when it came seemed incredibly old and weary, harsh and dry in the headphones.

"Be quiet."

So she was quiet while they waited for the other ship to appear. She felt uneasy just drifting through space like this. They were still travelling fast by most people's standards, about $\frac{1}{8}c$, but the slackening of their pace caused her to feel an unexpected anxiety. She had not realised how much of their sanity had depended upon maintaining their maximum speed. However compelling the reason they were now wasting time. She wriggled in her seat.

Hours passed. It was now in the small hours according to their own local time. She kept drifting in and out of sleep. Periodically, she looked at her husband to see if he too was asleep but his face remained calm and expressionless.

At four o'clock she finally fell asleep. He tapped her visor gently but she merely turned her face away. She was in a deep sleep. He pressed buttons and deep in the leaden heart of the ship atomic motors were activated.

He pressed more buttons and outer shields opened up. He studied the laser screens, waiting for the potential to build up. Unconsciously his mouth took on the shape of a frozen grin. Twin streams of blue light formed parallel lines that would meet in infinity. There was a slight rustling sound in the ship. He took his finger off the button and the lasers cut out.

Well, he was not going to wait here like a rat in a trap. He unstrapped himself, lowered himself to the ground and walked down the spiral stairway.

Something awakened her. She looked at the screens; there was nothing untoward. She looked at her husband. He wasn't there. The couch beside her was empty. Some movement at her peripheral vision caused her to turn her head. She gazed at a black armoured figure, its face invisible under the black helmet. She gasped, her heart jolted, pounded, then a pinprick in her shoulder, the figure began to waver, seemed to fall away from her, black curtains were drawn across her vision.

It took him five minutes of careful movement to get his wife into the strait-jacket. Then he strapped her firmly into the couch and made sure that she was breathing comfortably. He picked up the control pack and keyed the weapon system to his own body armour. He was now a moving target. He dare not wait inside the ship. He would wait outside linked to the ship's oxygen and power until the last moment. He moved quickly now, clambered down into the house, down again to the elevator, then to the escape hatch. Five minutes later he was sitting in his harness floating a few feet from the black hull of the ship and, while motionless, invisible from thirty metres away.

Chapter 26

He floated like a child connected by the cords of oxygen and energy to a dark placenta. With his black carapace he looked like a huge beetle, grotesque and ungainly. He felt ridiculous and exhausted. Now it was he that ached to sleep, just a few minutes, only a few moments. He bit his tongue to keep awake and after a while the sleepiness passed. He had no great plans, but he knew the value of surprise, and if he could break into the other ship and get to its commander before they could get to him he reckoned he had a good chance of achieving something. It was as vague as that.

He had an hour's supply of lox attached to his chair for breathing once he had cut loose and his chemical power pack could move him about quite comfortably for about the same amount of time. He prided himself that he was quite good at this sort of thing. Once a flyer always a flyer. He reckoned he could hang about here for at least 24 hours before he would have to climb back and attend to his wife. Boy, would she be mad. He giggled. Nervous tension. Breathe deeply. The hysteria passed, leaving him depressed.

Because he really didn't know what was right. It would have been honourable to surrender his ship; what did his petty ambitions matter, what did his battle with his wife matter, what did anything to do with him matter in comparison with this extraordinary creation that he was waiting to meet. He just didn't like the way the thing was playing with him, the sense of deviousness, even furtiveness about it. And because of these peculiar provocations he had become a space warrior, had donned his armour and was ready to send laser swords by remote control into the belly of the enemy. Yes, he had elected to make it his enemy.

Suddenly, he felt very thirsty, his mouth felt dry. A gallon of fresh water was built into the harness and he took a sip and then another. He felt better. He cast his eyes about the heavens, noticed one bright star.

That seemed to be getting brighter. His heart began to beat faster. It was getting brighter and larger, traversing constellations, curving in on his position. It had a tiny shape. He cast off from the ship, the self-sealing connections popping as the valves closed. His power pack dropped him half a mile, a mile below his ship and he braked skilfully, hovered in position. The other ship was the size of an apricot held at arm's length, the size of an orange. It looked like a huge circular doughnut, a black hole in the middle. It was close enough to realise that he couldn't see the stars through the middle of the ship. It was lit up like a Christmas tree. It was at least fifty times the size of his own vehicle.

It had stopped a few miles from him, nevertheless it filled the heavens like a huge hollow sun. It was like sailing close to Jupiter. He was shaking in his armour but managed to operate the controls. He had to get aboard. He floated up invisible, the non-reflective surface of his armour causing him to appear as a shadow across the stars.

He was travelling quite fast now, aiming for the lower part of the circumference of the ship. He could see other human beings walking about in the lower chambers of the ship, he could see their faces. He saw two men talking to each other. He felt an almost irresistible desire to cry out to them. He was directly between the two ships, flying from one to the other.

He seemed to be flying for ever. Time seemed to stand still. He looked rearwards through the mirror that was fixed to his helmet. He could barely see his own ship. He braked and looked round. His ship was at least fifteen miles away. His enemy had retreated before his progress. Surely they hadn't spotted him? But the ship was still there in front of him, he could still see the men walking about in their chambers, their bodies pointing feet first towards the center of the black hole. He darted once more towards the men in the brightly lit chambers; he could see them talking, gesticulating, they appeared to be taking no notice of his own ship. He made no progress. He braked again, looked back, his ship was twenty, thirty miles behind him. He looked at his watch. He had been chasing this monster for half an hour.

Fury and frustration took hold of him. They were playing tricks with him. Well, the time of exploration had come to an end. This was it.

He pressed the buttons on the weapons control panel. Two brilliant beams appeared on each side of him – and the enemy ship disappeared.

He looked at empty space and felt, perhaps for the first time, its vast loneliness. He felt as if he had awakened from a long dream in which he and his wife had been the only participants. He knew then how ancient sailors must have felt after the Flying Dutchman had passed, he remembered the poem of the Ancient Mariner. Now, it had happened to him.

Sorrow filled him and the tears coursed down his face. He had never known it possible to feel such pain, every protuberance on the inside of his armour seemed to be sending daggers of agony through his body. And yet he knew he could not die. He turned round and floated back toward his ship.

Chapter 27

When he got back to the ship he untied his wife and apologised to her. She had been terrified, waiting in the dark for all the horrors she could think of. He told her that there was no other ship, that it was all imagination or wishful thinking. She began to weep then with such abandon that he realised that he was the messenger that brought news of total defeat. She clung to him sobbing like a little girl who has been struck, out of the blue, with bereavement. In near hysteria, she told him, desperately, that she had lost her only friends, they would never come back, that she might as well be dead. Then she was silent for a long time.

They did not speak for several hours. He turned up the lights, made coffee, emphasised normality. His wife wept again silently and copiously. Then she began to speak to him so quietly that he had to strain to hear.

She told him of the sorrows of her youth, of the loneliness she had experienced when she was growing up. The only person she had been able to talk to had been her brother, and when he had died the trap had finally closed. Only he had known of her misery and he had taken that news silent to his grave. After that she had sworn that she would honour his memory by never telling another soul of her agonies. For she had loved him utterly. She broke down again, unable to go on. He waited.

Then he, her husband, had told her of his decision to go into space; it had been like her brother dying all over again. Once again she was being deserted. She wondered if it was something she had done, that he should want to leave her; because she did not believe that he really wanted her to accompany him. But she allowed herself to be persuaded that he did, everybody was saying how heroic, how extraordinary they were, to sacrifice their lives for the sake of humanity.

And so she had played along with it. It had solved so many problems but then suicide always did. For that was what it had been for her. A drugged sleep for the rest of her life. And in sleep she had had dreams, people had visited her, Bill and Diana, no doubt others would come – all the friends she had never previously allowed into her life.

She felt that her husband's decision to travel to Esther had been a positive one, in part perhaps motivated by anger or frustration, but nevertheless his life had been in a sense saved by the expedition, it had been given a meaning. But her decision had been entirely negative, entirely escapist. It had been an avoidance technique on a gigantic scale. Her psychiatrist had practically told her so. She had come to hate her husband because she was jealous of him, because he was happy and she was not.

Did she still hate him?

Sometimes. And other times she realised that he was the only man she had ever loved with the exception of her brother.

"I don't think motives are necessarily that important. You can start the right thing for the wrong reasons and vice versa. Psychoanalysis implies an absolute truth. I don't think we're in a position to deal in absolutes. The only real question is whether we go on or go back."

"I want to go back. I know now I want children, our children, and I don't believe we have the right to sentence them to a life of isolation in space. If we were a space community like the one you've apparently just seen it would be different."

"You should have thought of that before you agreed to come."

"Yes, I should have. I did. I thought it wouldn't be important. I was wrong. Did you think about children before you made your decision? I don't think you did – that was why you were so desperate and afraid. That was why you couldn't face me, why you went out and walked the streets at four in the morning. Perhaps you were running away too."

He looked up at eEridani shining above them. They could make it, they would be old but they could make it. The first people to the stars. Tears filled his eyes.

"It's just a sun like our own. If there is a planet, it will be just a planet. One day people, a lot of people will go there. We're the scouts, darling, we're preparing the way. We've come further than anyone has come before. We're over seven years out. Next time it will be fifteen or twenty, ships will get faster, it's just a matter of time."

"But our mission will have failed. What will we have gained from an aborted mission, from this mission?"

"How about – to stay happy people need to take risks? We know now the biggest problem is not the dangers but the boredom. You can't put a couple, or a community in aspic and hope that it will survive for more than a few months. Nothing less than a city-state will survive the ride to Esther or anywhere else. That's the message we're bringing back."

Travelling in the infinite, they had run out of space, or perhaps out of time, because only through time can things change and grow, and out here there was less and less change. They had begun to see it in their own faces. They were getting older but they weren't changing. Slowly, infinitely slowly they were falling into the big sleep, a world of increasing lassitude, where movement and thought became slower and slower, where communication became harder and harder. Yes, they were becoming like angels, and only angels have wings, but angels are incapable of independent thought, they are only the messengers of Another. And deprived of the light, they were like fallen angels, immobile for all eternity, frozen in adoration or fear, it no longer mattered.

He smiled at his wife. She was so beautiful, he loved her so much.

"Let's go home."

She kissed him lightly on the mouth.

"Chicago."

Printed in Great Britain
by Amazon